哈福

哈福

I love writing~

# 英語寫作
## Writing Skill
# 滿分特訓

哇，英文寫作更順暢了！

**最有效的基礎英語寫作訓練**

施銘瑋／主編

Craig Sorenson／著

張中倩／譯

哈福

# 三十分鐘滿分特訓，英語寫作滿級分！

　　網路科技的發明與進步讓國際間互通的業務日趨繁雜，具有英語這項優勢，即是縮短了國與國之間的距離。無論是大如外交、商業往來，或小如旅遊、考試，懂英語，致勝籌碼就占的愈大。想要高人一等，享受美好的生活，有一份好工作或好學歷，參加NEW TOEIC、英語檢定、托福、統測、雅思…等等，各類英語鑑定考試，都是必要過程，證明自己的英語實力。

　　因應時代的需求，英語強調全方位發展，聽、説、讀、寫能力，都不容忽視。而這其中，又以寫作更為不易。寫作講求精確、有組織性。以英語寫作，除了對文字的運用難以道地、流暢外，更有中文所沒有的大大小小的文法問題。

　　本書特聘專業美語老師為讀者編撰的「英語寫作滿分特訓」，內容包括寫作主題、寫作問答與寫作改正三個部份。除了精心設計符合考試趨勢的題型外，各種題型更附上多篇作者嚴謹編寫的答案範例，供讀者參考模擬，寫作功力輕鬆提升。

　　寫作除了要注意邏輯、通順度、及組織架構外，英語寫作更多了三項必需注意的重點，即文法、字彙及標點符號。這三大要點看似簡單，但若因此而不在意，往往會變成通往寫作高分的最大絆腳石，因為這正顯示了您的英語功力夠不夠紮實。本書教您有技巧地避免這些錯誤，先打好用字遣辭的實力，再跟著本書有系統地訓練寫作應答訣竅、文章組織結構，發展張力十足的內容，讓您寫作無障礙，考試不焦慮！

　　「英語寫作滿分特訓」精選實用題型，針對各項英語寫作測驗常考的主題、類型歸納編撰測驗題，精闢分析各類題型解題方式，考試作答更快速。本書精彩內容包括：

　　**1. 寫作主題**　本單元訓練您對文章的架構、故事情節的舖陳的寫作技巧，每篇主題文章先引出故事的起頭，要您接續寫出結尾。讓您腦力激盪，開發創意潛能，寫出最有力的文章結尾。

　　**2. 寫作問答**　根據常考題型設計而成的題目，配合考試趨勢，搭配作者提供的精彩寫作範例，讓您在最有限的時間內，抓住寫作訣竅，培養寫作組織能力，迅速練成下筆成章的功力。

　　**3. 寫作改正**　藉由精選文章，設下各種常犯錯誤的陷阱，訓練您對英語的敏銳度。並於文章之後附上答案解析，讓您更能掌握英語用字的原則，提升英語寫作的精確度，輕鬆拿到寫作高分。

　　在開始進行寫作訓練前，請先熟讀第一部份作者提供的寫作小秘訣（Writing Tips），在寫作時，若能時時掌握這些原則，就能輕輕鬆鬆考試高分。接著再仔細研讀習作本書的題型，充分把握各類寫作的解題方式，對於各類寫作考試，都可迎刃而解，突破高分，在競爭激烈的環境中脫穎而出。

編者　謹識

Hello and welcome! This book will help you practice your English writing skills. It's a very good idea to practice writing because nearly all English tests, including the GEPT, NEW TOEIC...., have sections that require you to write English compositions.

Most students say that the writing part of English tests is more difficult than the reading, speaking or listening parts of English tests. Why is this so? There are two main reasons. First, when you are asked to write an English essay, you will need to compose it yourself. The grammar, vocabulary and structure of the essay will all come from you. This is different from other tests where you only need to choose the correct answer from several answer choices.

The second reason that this is a difficult part of English tests is that after you write, you will also need to edit your composition. Editing is when you look over your essay to find and correct mistakes. All writers must do this, even native English speakers! So remember, after you finish writing a section in English, you should always go back and check for mistakes. Usually, if you cannot find any mistakes that only means that you haven't looked closely enough! The last section of this book is designed to help you learn to find and correct some of the most common mistakes in English writing.

✐ So get your pencil and eraser ready, it's time to begin!

嗨！這本書將幫助你練習英文寫作技巧。我們應該練習寫作，因為幾乎所有的英文考試，包括GEPT, NEW TOEIC....，都有寫作的部分。

大多數學生都表示英文考試的寫作部分比閱讀、口語或聽力要困難許多。為什麼會這樣呢？這主要有兩個原因。第一，當你得寫英文作文時，你需要自己創作。文法、字彙與作文的結構都必須來自你自己。這不同於其他考試，因為在其他考試中，你只需要在數個答案中選出正確答案即可。

寫作困難的第二個原因，是因為當你寫好作文後，你還得要編審自己的作品。編審是指你需要檢查自己的作文，來找出錯誤、並加以更正。所有寫作者都必須這樣做，就算是以英文為母語的人也不例外。所以你要記住，在你寫完一部分的英文之後，你必須重複檢查是否有錯誤。通常，如果你找不出任何錯誤，這都只意謂著你檢查得不夠仔細。本書最後一個部分的目標，在於幫助你學習如何找出並更正一些英文寫作中最常犯的錯誤。

✍ 所以準備好你的鉛筆和橡皮擦，開始吧！

# 目錄
## CONTENTS

## Part 1 Writing Topics 寫作主題

## Part 2 Writing Answers 寫作問答

**Part 3** **Writing Corrections** **寫作改正**

**Part 4** **Appendix 附錄**

- Trust your hopes and not your fears.
  （相信你的希望，拒絕你的恐懼。）

- Never say die.
  （永不放棄。）

- Things at the worst will mend.
  （事情再糟也能彌補。）

- Idleness is the key of beggary.
  （懶惰是貧窮的主要因素。）

- A rolling stone gathers no moss.
  （滾石不生苔。／轉業不聚財。）

Part

1

# Writing Topics
寫作主題

For this part of the writing test you will be asked to complete a story. These writing questions always begin with a paragraph that tells you the start of a story and then you must write the ending. Here are some points to remember:

✍ Before you start writing, you should read and reread the first paragraph to make sure you fully understand the topic. If you don't understand the beginning of the story how would you be able to write the ending? It isn't necessary to understand every detail, but you should have a general idea about the plot.

✍ When you read the beginning of the story, take note of these important details: the characters' names, the place where the story happens, the problem or situation that occurs in the story, and

# 寫作小技巧

　　在這部分的寫作測驗中，你必須要完成一個故事。這些寫作題目都從一個段落開始，告訴你故事的起頭，然後你必須將故事寫完。以下有幾個重點要謹記：

✍ 在你開始寫作之前，你必須詳細反覆閱讀第一個段落，確定你完全瞭解主題。如果你不瞭解故事的開始，又怎能將其敘述完全呢？當然，你沒有必要完全瞭解每一個細節，但必須清楚大致的故事發展。

✍ 當你閱讀故事開頭時，要對下列這些重要細節特別注意：主角的名字、故事發生的地點、故事中發生的問題或情境，及故事的寫作時態（過去式、現在式或未來式）。

the tense (past, present,future) in which the story is written.

✍ Think of a simple ending for the story. This is the part that allows you to be creative. Remember, you will be graded on the structure and composition of your writing, so the start and end of each question should be logically connected. If, like the first essay below, the story begins with a problem in the zoo, then the ending you write should resolve this problem in the zoo.

✍ English writing tests are always graded on the correct use of the following five points: grammar, vocabulary, punctuation, content, and organization. Below is a checklist with questions that you can use to help you write and edit your compositions. We recommend that you use this checklist to look for mistakes in your essays. If you practice using this list, then you can become a good

✍ 想像一個簡單的故事結尾。這個部分你可以自行發揮。要記住，評分著重在你的文章架構與內容，所以每個問題的開始與結尾，都必須具邏輯的連貫性。如果像下面的第一篇文章，其故事開頭是在動物園裡發生的問題，你所寫的結尾，就該與解決這個動物園裡的問題有關。

✍ 英文寫作測驗的評分，都以下列五點的正確與否為基準，包括：文法、字彙、標點符號、內容與組織。下面這個檢查清單中，列出一些可以幫助你寫作及編審自己的文章。建議你利用這個檢查清單，找出你作文中的錯誤。如果你練習使用這份清單，那你就會成為檢視你自己作品的好編審，進而在英文考試中得高分。記住下面五個要點：

editor of your own work. And this will lead to much better scores on English tests! Remember these five important points:

## ❶ Grammar

Do you use the right verb tenses? If the story begins in the past tense, then you should continue writing it in the past tense. Do the subject and verb agree in tense? Do you correctly use conjunctions (and, but, or...) and prepositions (about, before, under...)? Do you only use adverbs to modify verbs and adjectives to modify nouns?

## ❷ Vocabulary

Do you use a variety of words in your answer? Do you use many words that weren't in the question? Writing English compositions is a good time to show off some of the

## ❶文法

　　你所使用的動詞時態是否正確？如果故事以過去式開始，你便應該用過去式，把故事寫完。另外，主詞與動詞時態是否一致？有沒有正確使用連接詞（像是and, but, or…）與介係詞（像是about, before, under…）？你是否只用副詞修飾動詞、形容詞修飾名詞？

## ❷字彙

　　你的答案中是否使用許多不同的字彙？你是否使用許多在問題中沒有出現的字彙？英文寫作是個讓你可以炫耀一下你所學的字彙的好時機。你是否正確使用字彙，讓讀的人清楚知道你對這

vocabulary you've learned. Do you use the words correctly to show that you know what they mean? Of course, whenever you use a new vocabulary word, you should make certain that you use it correctly.

## ❸ Punctuation

Do you know how to use periods, commas, question marks, and apostrophes? Are your sentences correctly punctuated? Or does your essay have many very long sentences with no punctuation? It is usually better to write several shorter sentences than to write one long sentence. It's easier to make mistakes with long sentences, and easier to avoid mistakes with short sentences.

些字的瞭解程度？當然，每當你使用新字時，都要確定是否有正確地使用。

### ❸標點符號

　　你知道什麼時候該用句點、逗點、問號和撇號嗎？你的句子是否都正確地標上標點符號？你的作文中是否有過多的長句，卻沒有標點符號？通常寫幾個短句，比寫一個長句要適當的多。因為寫長句容易出錯，而短句則容易避免犯錯。

## ❹ Content

Does your essay address the issue or problem described in the question? Did you write an ending to the story that is suitable to the beginning? Does your ending seem connected to the beginning? None of these will be problems if you remember to understand the topic before you begin writing.

## ❺ Organization

Is your essay organized in a clear, logical way? A well-written essay will have a clear progression from beginning to middle to end.

## ❹內容

你所寫的文章是否與題目闡述的問題有關？你所寫的故事結尾是否符合開頭的發展？你的故事結尾是否和開頭相關？如果你記得要在開始寫作前，瞭解主題的話，以上這些都不成問題。

## ❺組織架構

你的作文組織是否清楚、符合邏輯？一篇好的作文，從開始、中段到結尾，都要有清楚的發展。

## Instructions

Please read the paragraph below and write an ending to the story. You should use between ten and fifteen sentences to write an ending that is suitable for this story.

## 寫作指示

　　請閱讀下面的段落，然後寫出故事的結尾。你應使用十到十五個句子，寫出一個適合這個故事的結局。

# Writing Topic Number 1

| Title | **A Problem at the Zoo** |

One day Lisa and her little sister Sarah went to the zoo. It was a Saturday and the zoo was very busy and crowded with people. After they looked at the elephants, the two girls went to see the monkeys. Sarah was very excited because she had never before seen a real monkey.

When they got to the place with the monkeys, Lisa turned around to tell Sarah. But Sarah wasn't there! Lisa could not find her sister. Lisa was very worried and she started to look for her sister.

# 寫作主題一

## 主題　在動物園發生的難題

　　有一天，麗莎和妹妹莎拉去動物園，那天是週六，動物園裡人非常多。在她們看完大象後，兩個女生接著去看猴子。莎拉很興奮，因為她從來沒有看過真的猴子。

　　當她們到了猴子區後，麗莎轉身要告訴莎拉她們到了，但是莎拉不見了！麗莎找不到妹妹，她很擔心，於是開始到處去找妹妹。

## Example Answer 1

Lisa was very scared. Where did Sarah go? Lisa walked back to the elephant area to see if her sister was there. She wasn't! So Lisa ran back to the place with the monkeys. There were many people there and it was difficult for Lisa to see very far.

But then she heard a noise. It was a little girl crying. Lisa turned around and saw that it was Sarah! Sarah was sitting on a bench and crying to herself. Lisa ran over and hugged her sister.

She was so happy to see her again! Now she would be very careful and always hold her sister's hand.

## 範例解答一

麗莎很害怕，莎拉倒底跑到哪裡去了？麗莎回到大象區，去看看妹妹是否在那裡，但莎拉不在那裡！於是麗莎跑回猴子區。那裡的人很多，所以麗莎沒辦法看得很遠。

但那時，她聽到了一個聲音，是小女孩的哭聲。麗莎轉身，看到那個哭泣的女孩是莎拉。莎拉坐在一個長椅上，一個人哭泣。麗莎跑過去，抱住了妹妹。

她好高興再次看到妹妹。現在，她會很小心，總是牽著妹妹的手。

## Example Answer 2

Where was little Sarah? Lisa started to shout her sister's name. "Sarah! Sarah! Where are you?"she said.

Just then a policeman heard Lisa and came over to talk to her. Lisa told the policeman about the problem and he said he would help look for Sarah. Then, the two of them walked around the area with the monkeys. But they didn't see Sarah!

At last, the policeman suggested they go back to the elephant area to look for her. As they were walking back, Lisa felt something pulling at her shirt. She turned around. It was little Sarah! The two sisters were very happy to see each other again.

They thanked the policeman and then went back to look at the monkeys.

## 範例解答二

　　小莎拉人在哪裡？麗莎大聲叫著妹妹的名字，她說：「莎拉、莎拉，妳在哪裡？」

　　在這個時候，一個警察聽到麗莎的叫聲，走過來和她談話。麗莎告訴警察她的難題，警察說他會幫忙找尋莎拉。後來，他們兩個人在猴子區走來走去，但沒看到莎拉。

　　最後，那位警察建議回到大象區去找莎拉。在他們走回去的路上，麗莎感到有東西在拉她的裙子，她轉身查看，是小莎拉！她們兩姊妹很高興再次見到彼此。

　　她們向警察道謝，然後又走回去看猴子了。

# Writing Topic Number 2

## Title　Car Troubles

Jeremy was very excited. This was his first time driving alone. He was using his father's car to drive to another town to see his old friend Bob.

Jeremy was driving on a highway and had to drive about 200 kilometers to get to his friend's house. Everything was going fine until Jeremy heard a noise.

Bang! What was that? It sounded like the car had a problem. Jeremy was worried, but he continued driving.

Then, about ten minutes later, Jeremy saw something strange. It was smoke! There was smoke coming out of the car!

# 寫作主題二

## 主題　車子問題

　　傑若米非常興奮，這是他第一次單獨一人開車。他開著爸爸的車到另一個城鎮，去看他的老朋友鮑伯。

　　傑若米開上了高速公路，他得要開大約二百公里的路，才到得了他朋友家。一切都很順利，直到傑若米聽到一個聲響。

　　砰！這是怎麼回事？聽起來好像是車子有問題。傑若米很擔心，但他繼續開車。

　　然後大約十分鐘後，傑若米看到很怪的事，他看到了煙，車子正在冒煙！

## Example Answer 1

Jeremy had never seen a car smoke before and he didn't know what he should do. He started driving more slowly. But the car was still smoking! He drove even slower, but the car continued to smoke.

Finally, he decided that he must park the car. He drove to the side of the road and turned the car off. After a few minutes, the smoke stopped coming out of the car.

Jeremy used his phone to call his father. He told his father where he was, and his father said he would send someone there to help fix the car. Jeremy waited in the car for help to arrive.

## 範例解答一

傑若米從來沒有看過車子冒煙,他不知道應該怎麼做才好。他開始慢慢地開,但車子仍在冒煙。他把速度放的更慢,但車子仍在冒煙。

最後,他決定必須把車停下來。他把車子開到路邊,然後熄火。幾分鐘後,車子停止冒煙了。

傑若米用他的電話打給爸爸,告訴爸爸他人在哪裡,他爸爸說他會叫人去幫忙修車。傑若米在車子裡等待援助的到來。

## Example Answer 2

Jeremy became very worried. What was the problem? Would his father be angry? Jeremy knew that he had to stop the car and turn off the engine.

He found a gas station and turned in. He turned off the car and went to talk to the man at the gas station. He told the man the problem and the man went over to look at the car.

"Your car is too hot," said the man "You need to put in some water." Then, the man helped Jeremy put water in the car. After that, Jeremy thanked the man and drove away.

Jeremy was very relieved that the car was not broken, and very soon he would arrive at his friend's house.

## 範例解答二

　　傑若米非常擔心，到底是怎麼了？爸爸會生氣嗎？傑若米知道自己必須把車停下來，並熄掉引擎。

　　他找到一個加油站，轉了進去。他把車子熄了火，去和加油站的人談話。他把自己的麻煩告訴那個人，那個人便和他一起去看車子。

　　他說：「你的車子過熱，你需要加些水。」然後，那個人幫忙傑若米在車子裡加了水。後來，傑若米向那個人道謝，便開車離開了。

　　傑若米知道車子沒壞掉後，心中放心多了。很快，他就可以到朋友家了。

# Writing Topic Number 3

**Title** | **The Dark House**

Yi-wen was a college student and she lived together with her four roommates in a big house. The house was very close to their college, only about a ten minute walk.

One day, after finishing her classes for the day, Yi-wen started walking home. Her friends finished earlier and they would all be waiting for her at home. Today, was Yi-wen's birthday and they had all planned to go out to dinner to celebrate.

But when Yi-wen got close to her house she noticed something strange. The house was very dark. None of the lights, inside or outside, were turned on.

# 寫作主題三

## 主題　暗暗的房子

　　怡雯是一個大學生，她和四個室友一起住在一個大房子裡。這個房子離她們的學校很近，走路大約只要十分鐘。

　　有一天，在她上完課後，怡雯開始走路回家。她的朋友們比較早下課，都會在家裡等她。那天是她的生日，大家計畫好了要外出用餐慶祝。

　　但是當怡雯快到家的時候，她注意到有件事很奇怪，她們的房子很暗，房子裡外都沒有任何燈光。

## Example Answer 1

Yi-wen started to get worried. Where were her friends? Did they forget that today was her birthday? Yi-wen walked up the steps to the front of the house. She was trying to be very quiet. She listened but could hear no sound coming from inside the house.

Slowly, she opened the front door and went inside. Suddenly, the lights turned on and all of her friends jumped out! "Surprise! Happy Birthday Yi-wen!" all her friends shouted together.

It was a surprise birthday party! Her friends had not forgotten her birthday after all.

## 範例解答一

　　怡雯開始擔心。她的朋友們跑到哪裡去了？難道她們忘記今天是她的生日了嗎？怡雯走上了房子前的臺階。她試著盡量安靜，注意聆聽，卻聽不到房子裡有任何聲響。

　　她慢慢地打開前門，走進屋裡。突然，燈光全亮了，她的朋友們全都跑出來，一起大聲喊：「驚喜！怡雯，生日快樂！」

　　那是一個驚喜生日派對！她的朋友們終究沒忘記她的生日。

## Example Answer 2

Yi-wen started thinking to herself. "Where are my friends? Did they forget that today is my birthday?" She was a little sad when she went to open the front door.

She went inside the house and turned on the lights. Nobody was there! Yi-wen was feeling very bad and she went to her room to put her books away. Then, she saw something. There was a note on her bedroom door. Yi-wen walked over to look at the note.

It said, "Sorry, Yi-wen, we had to leave early to go buy you a birthday present. We'll meet you at the restaurant at 7 o'clock. Happy Birthday!" Yi-wen was very relieved.

## 範例解答二

　　怡雯心裡開始想：「我的朋友們跑到哪裡去了？難道她們忘記今天是我生日了嗎？」當她走去開前門時，她有一點感傷。

　　她走進屋裡，打開電燈。一個人都沒有！怡雯感覺很糟，她走到自己的房間去放書。然後她看到一樣東西，她房間門上有一張紙條，怡雯走過去看那張紙條。

　　紙條上寫著：「抱歉，怡雯，我們得早點出發，去買妳的生日禮物。我們七點鐘會在餐廳和妳碰面。生日快樂！」怡雯鬆了一口氣。

# Writing Topic Number 4

| Title | The Missing Dog |
| --- | --- |

Nikki was a very happy girl. Yesterday was her twelfth birthday and her parents had given her a puppy dog as a birthday present. She named the dog Skippy and spent all day playing with it.

The next day, when Nikki came home from school, she went to her room to find Skippy. But Skippy wasn't there! Nikki was worried and started to look around the house for her dog. But she still couldn't find it! She started to get very worried.

"Skippy! Skippy! Where are you? Skippy!" she shouted.

# 寫作主題四

## 主題 走失的狗

妮琪是一個快樂的女孩。昨天是她的十二歲生日，她的父母送她一隻小狗當做生日禮物。她把小狗命名為史奇普，整天和牠一起玩。

隔日，當妮琪放學回家後，她去自己的房間找尋史奇普，但牠不在房裡。妮琪很擔心，開始在房子四周找尋她的狗。可是她仍然找不到。於是她變得很擔心了。

她大叫著：「史奇普！你在哪裡？史奇普！」

## Example Answer 1

Nikki looked everywhere for her dog. She looked in the kitchen, she looked in the bathroom and she looked in the living room. But she couldn't find Skippy anywhere.

"Skippy! Come here! Skippy!" she said. But the dog did not come. "Oh no! This is terrible,"she thought, "I only had my dog for one day and now he is gone!" Nikki was very sad and she sat down on her bed and started to cry.

Then, she felt something touch her leg. It was wet and cold. She looked down and saw Skippy! He was touching her leg with his nose. Poor little Skippy was hiding under Nikki's bed. She picked him up and kissed him and said, "Skippy, I am so happy I found you again!"

## 範例解答一

　　妮琪到處找她的狗。她去了廚房、浴室及客廳，但到處都找不到史奇普。

　　她叫著：「史奇普！過來這裡，史奇普！」但狗兒沒有過來。她心想：「天啊！這太可怕了。我才擁有這隻狗一天而已，現在牠居然不見了。」妮琪非常難過，她坐在自己的床上，開始哭泣。

　　然後，她感覺到有個東西在碰觸她的腳，濕濕冷冷的。她往下一看，看到了史奇普，牠正在用鼻子碰觸她的腳。可憐的小史奇普躲在妮琪的床下。她把小狗抱起來，親親牠，並說：「史奇普，我好高興我找到你了。」

Part 1

寫作 Writing Topics

## Example Answer 2

But she didn't see Skippy. Nikki looked around her house one more time but couldn't find her dog. Then, she sat down at the table and started to think. "Where could Skippy be? He doesn't seem to be in the house."

She was starting to get very worried when the phone rang. "Hello", said Nikki. It was her mother on the phone. Nikki said, "Mom, I just came home from school and I can't find Skippy! He must have been stolen! What can I do?"

"Don't worry!" said her mother, "Skippy is here with me. I took him to the park to go for a walk. We're coming home now." Nikki said goodbye to her mother and sat down. She felt much better. Skippy wasn't lost. He would be coming home very soon.

## 範例解答二

但是她沒看到史奇普。妮琪又在房子周圍找了一遍，還是沒有找到她的狗。然後，她在桌旁坐下，開始思考：「史奇普會在哪裡呢？牠好像不在屋子裡。」

正當她開始擔心時，電話響了起來。妮琪回答說：「喂？」是媽媽打來的電話。妮琪說：「媽，我剛從學校回來，我找不到史奇普。牠一定是被偷走了。我該怎麼辦才好呢？」

媽媽說：「別擔心，史奇普和我在一起，我帶牠到公園散散步，現在正要回家了。」妮琪和媽媽道再見後，坐了下來，心中感到好多了。史奇普沒丟掉，牠馬上就會回來了。

# Writing Topic Number 5

| Title | Not Enough Money |
|---|---|

Lisa was 17 years old and had a brother and sister. She was the oldest child in her family and had just started working a new job. Because she had a job of her own she also had some pocket money.

One day, she decided to do something nice for her brother and sister. She wanted to take them out to eat ice cream. But when they got to the ice cream store, Lisa realized she had a problem. She didn't bring enough money!

She knew her brother and sister would be very sad if they didn't get to eat ice cream. What could she do?

# 寫作主題五

## 主題　錢不夠

　　麗莎十七歲，有一個弟弟和妹妹。她是家中最大的小孩，剛剛開始一份新工作。因為她有自己的工作，所以有一些零用錢。

　　有一天，她決定要為她的弟妹做些事情，她想要帶他們去吃冰淇淋。但是當他們到了冰淇淋店時，麗莎知道她碰上了一個問題，她沒帶夠錢。

　　她知道如果弟妹們吃不到冰淇淋，他們會很失望，她應該怎麼做才好？

## Example Answer 1

Lisa looked in her wallet and saw that she only had 10 dollars. But each ice cream cost at least 5 dollars. She didn't have enough money for all three of them to get ice cream. But Lisa was a nice girl who loved her brother and sister very much. She decided that this time she would buy each of them an ice cream and not get one for herself.

She helped her brother and sister order the ice cream and then they went to sit down at the table. Lisa watched her brother and sister eating their ice cream and saw how happy they were. This made Lisa feel very good and she didn't care that she didn't have an ice cream for herself.

After they finished eating, the three children went home. Lisa told her mother what had happened and her mother said "Lisa, you really are an excellent older sister!"

## 範例解答一

　　麗莎看看自己的錢包，只有十塊錢，但每個冰淇淋至少要五塊錢。她的錢不夠買三人份的冰淇淋。因為麗莎是個很好的女孩，她很愛弟弟妹妹，所以她決定這次她要幫弟妹們各買一個冰淇淋，而不買給自己。

　　她幫弟弟妹妹點了冰淇淋，然後他們走到桌邊坐了下來。看著弟弟妹妹快樂地吃著冰淇淋，讓麗莎感到很高興，她並不介意自己沒有冰淇淋可吃。

　　吃完冰淇淋後，他們三個人就回家了。麗莎告訴媽媽事情的經過，媽媽說：「麗莎，妳真是個很棒的姊姊。」

## Example Answer 2

Lisa felt embarrassed that she didn't bring enough money. She looked at the menu and saw that all of the ice cream cost at least 5 dollars. Then, she had an idea.

Although she couldn't buy three ice creams, one for each of them, she could buy one very big ice cream and the three of them could share it. And that is what she did. She ordered the largest ice cream that the store had. It was very, very big. Then, Lisa and her brother and sister went to eat the ice cream. It was delicious!

When they finished eating, Lisa's brother and sister said, "Thanks, Lisa! You are the best sister in the whole world."

## 範例解答二

麗莎為自己沒有帶足夠的錢，感到很尷尬。她看著點菜單，知道一個冰淇淋至少要五元，於是她想到一個主意。

雖然她沒有足夠的錢，為他們三個人各買一個冰淇淋，她可以點大份的冰淇淋，三個人一起吃。於是她便這麼做了。她點了一份店裡最大的冰淇淋，份量真的很多。然後，麗莎和弟弟妹妹把冰淇淋吃了，真的很好吃。

當他們吃完後，麗莎的弟弟妹妹說：「麗莎，謝謝。妳是世界上最好的姊姊。」

- Do business, but be not a slave to it.
  （做事，但不要做事務的奴隸。）

- Cut your coat according to your cloth.
  （量力而為。）

- Better rely on yourself than on others.
  （求人不如求己。）

- Whatever you do, do it well.
  （無論做什麼，做好它！）

- Whatever you do, do with all your might.
  （不管做什麼，都要盡心盡力。）

# Part

2

# Writing Answers
## 寫作問答

## Instructions

For this part of the test, you will be asked to write answers to questions. Each topic will usually have several small questions. You should read all of the questions, see how they connect to each other, and then write an answer that addresses all of them.

Remember! Each topic will have several interrelated questions and your written answer should bring the answers to each question together.

## 寫作指示

　　在考試的這個部分，你需要針對問題，寫出答案。每一個主題通常有好幾個小問題。你應該要把所有問題讀一遍，看看它們之間的關係，然後寫出一個可以回答全部問題的答案。

　　要記住，每一個主題會有好幾個相關問題，你的寫作答案必須將它們串連起來。

## Writing Question Number 1

### 寫作問題一

• Please use approximately 110 to 160 words to answer the question.
請使用大約110~160個字，來回答問題。

**Question** Have you ever been frightened? When were you frightened? What scared you and what did you do about it?

**問題** 你有沒有很害怕過？你何時感到害怕？什麼東西嚇到了你？你又是如何應付該情況？

## 文章開始 Start From Here

學 習 小 撇 步

## 衝過學習瓶頸‧英語輕鬆拿高分

PART I 寫作篇

　　國內的英語學習人口，多半是「讀」、「寫」能力優於「聽」、「説」能力。但是，也有些人對寫作一竅不通；試想，當英語文章不通順、無條理時，您怎能寫出一篇打動人心的英文履歷表呢？各式英檢的寫作測驗，光憑著一口溜英語上陣，也絕對是讓人貽笑大方。那麼，面對寫作，我們該如何衝破心理障礙與學習瓶頸呢？

　　首先，您務必要累積足夠的字彙量與文法概念，並經常練習。嘗試將自己的想法，轉換成英語，寫在本子裡，並請信賴的老師或同好閱讀。甚至，您也可以跟朋友組成寫作團隊，每週互相交換作品。這種做法的優點是，朋友的互相督促與鼓勵，可以減少「三天打魚，兩天曬網」的懈怠症狀，而彼此的良性互動，更能激發出正向積極的競爭心態。不知不覺間，大家的英語寫作程度都快速提升了！

　　另外，也可以藉由抄寫英語文章、歌詞，提升自己對單字的熟悉度與親切感，也能因此多得到優美句子與諺語的滋養。英檢考試時，寫出來的文章，自然高人一等，讓人眼睛一亮！

Writing Answers 寫作問答

## Example Answer 1

I have been scared before. It happened last year when my friends and I went to the mountains. We had been hiking up a trail on a mountain for three hours. There were no houses, no stores and no other people near us. We were all alone in the forest.

Then, we noticed that one of our friends, Stacy, was not with us! We all got scared and worried. Where did Stacy go? We started looking for her. Some of us went up the trail and others went back down. We looked for two hours and it started to get dark.

It was becoming night and we still hadn't found our friend. We were all very worried when we suddenly heard a noise. It was someone shouting! It was Stacy! She had taken a wrong turn and separated from the group. We were all happy to see her again, and we were all very careful after that.

## 範例解答一

　　我以前曾經被嚇到過。事情發生在去年，當時，我朋友和我去爬山。那時我們已經在山上的步道上健行了三個鐘頭，附近沒有房子、商店或人煙，森林裡只有我們。

　　然後，我們發現我們的一個朋友—— 史黛西，已經走散了。大家都感到很害怕、擔心。史黛西到底跑到哪裡去了？我們開始找尋她。有些人往前走，有些人回頭去找。我們找了兩個小時，天色也開始變暗。

　　夜晚來臨了，我們還是沒找到我們的朋友。大家感到很擔心時，突然間聽到了一個聲音。是一個人大叫的聲音 —— 那是史黛西。她轉錯了一個彎，和整群人走散了。我們都很高興再見到她，之後，我們大家都很小心。

# Example Answer 2

The last time I was really frightened was when I was eight years old. My brother and I went to visit our uncle in the country. He lives alone in a big house in the middle of a forest.

When my brother and I got to his house, we didn't see my uncle. We opened the front door and went inside. The house was all dark inside. My brother and I walked in. Then, my brother suddenly ran up the stairs to the second floor. I was all alone in this big, dark house. I was very scared. I started looking for the lights.

Then, I heard a noise, like this "Jeeeeerrrry!" It sounded like a ghost calling my name! I was so scared I started to cry. Then, all of the lights in the house turned on.

There was my brother and uncle and they were both laughing at me! They were only joking with me.

## 範例解答二

　　我上一次真正感到害怕，是在我八歲的時候。我哥哥和我去鄉下探訪我們的舅舅。他獨自一人住在森林中的大房子裡。

　　當哥哥和我到達他的房子時，卻沒有看到舅舅。我們打開前門，走進屋裡。屋子裡面一片漆黑。哥哥和我走了進去。然後，我哥哥突然跑上二樓，於是我便獨自一人在這個寬大、黑暗的房子裡。我很害怕，所以我開始找尋電燈。

　　之後，我聽到一個聲音，聽起來像是：「傑傑傑傑傑瑞。」聽起來好像是鬼在叫我的名字。我嚇得哭了起來，然後，屋裡的電燈全都亮了。

　　我哥哥和舅舅站在那裡，他們都在笑我，他們只是在和我開玩笑。

## Example Answer 3

When I was a little girl I was scared of everything. If I saw a big dog, I would get scared. If I heard a strange noise, I would get scared. If my teacher got angry at me, I would get scared.

Then, when I was a little older, I stopped being so afraid of things. My father told me once, "What doesn't kill you can only make you stronger." This means that sometimes it is good to get scared of things because it will make you a stronger person. Maybe something can scare you once, twice, or even three times, but after that you will have learned not to be afraid of that thing.

I think my father was right because now I am a stronger person and never really get scared anymore.

## 範例解答三

當我還是個小女孩時，我害怕每件事。如果我看到一隻大狗，我會害怕。如果我聽到奇怪的聲音，我會害怕。如果老師生我的氣，我也會害怕。

後來我大了點，便不再對事事感到害怕。我父親曾經告訴過我：「凡是殺不死你的事物，都會讓你變得更為堅強。」這句話的意思是：有時候害怕事物是件好事，因為這會讓你變得更堅強。也許一件事會嚇到你一次、兩次、甚至三次，但之後你就會學到不再懼怕那件事。

我想我父親是對的，因為現在我是個堅強的人，不再感到懼怕。

08

## Writing Question Number 2

### 寫作問題二

- Please use approximately 110 to 160 words to answer the question.

  請使用大約110～160個字，來回答問題。

**Question** What is your favorite class in school? Why do you like this subject? What do you think is interesting about it?

**問題** 你在學校裡最喜歡上什麼課？為什麼喜歡這個科目？你覺得它有什麼有趣之處？

文章開始　Start From Here

# Learning Skills
學 習 小 撇 步

## 衝過學習瓶頸・英語輕鬆拿高分

PART II　閱讀篇

許多「英語人」之所以遇到瓶頸，是因為閱讀量不夠，使進步程度受阻。還記得我們剛接觸英語時，每讀到一篇文章，總是在上面畫滿紅線，寫滿了單字的中譯？曾幾何時，我們已經不再查單字了？沒錯，問題就出在這裡！

閱讀的好處是累積式的。它不像聽力、口說，一旦停止接觸，就要回到原點，從新開始。閱讀，即使中斷一些時間，文字與感觸仍會刻印在我們心中。但也因為這樣，我們常忽略了閱讀對進步的重要　，因此使自己的程度無法突破。

要增加閱讀實力的最好方法，就是要廣泛閱讀各式文章。若是剛開始培養閱讀習慣的人，可以先從自己有興趣的主題下手。等到習慣養成後，再涉獵各式題材。不要侷限主題，這樣才能學到不同文體、句型、文字的運用。而這最大的好處，莫過於參加英檢考試時，各種閱讀測驗都難不倒您！

有深厚的興趣作根基，就如熬了一鍋好湯底，無論用任何新方法，或加任何新素材，保證道道都是又香又Ｑ的好料理，學習英語也一樣，方法對了，就能迅速打好根基，英語能力自然而然就提升了。

# Example Answer 1

My favorite class in school is history. I have been interested in history for many years, ever since I was a little boy. I'm interested in history for several reasons.

First, I think history is like reading stories from a long time ago. Some of these stories are very interesting. I like reading about the people of ancient Egypt most. The Egyptians were one of the world's first big civilizations. I also like studying history because it can teach you so many things.

If we study history carefully we can learn from the mistakes of the past. This will help our world to be a better place because we can avoid making the same mistakes again. These are the reasons that history is my favorite subject in school.

## 範例解答一

　　我在學校裡最喜歡上的課是歷史。自從孩童時代起，多年來，我一直對歷史很感興趣。我喜歡歷史的原因有好幾個。

　　首先，我覺得念歷史就像在讀很久以前發生的故事。有些故事非常有趣，我最喜歡讀古埃及的人物史，埃及是世界上最大的古文明之一。我喜歡讀歷史也是因為它可以教導我們許多事物。

　　如果我們仔細研究歷史，我們可以從過去的錯誤中學習。這可以幫助這個世界變得更美好，因為我們可以避免再犯同樣的錯誤。這些都是歷史是我最喜歡的學校科目的原因。

## Example Answer 2

The school subject that I like the most is math. Many people think that math is boring and difficult, but I think it is fun and easy.

Why do I like math? In math, you can always tell if you have the right answer or not. With some subjects, like English or history, it can be difficult to know if your answer is correct.

But with math, if you find an answer, you can usually check to see if it is correct. If it's not correct, you can change it until you find the right answer. Another reason I like math is that it is a very useful subject. If you are good at math, you can do many things and find many good jobs.

When I get older, I want to work as an engineer so math will be very useful for me when I need to find a job.

## 範例解答二

　　我在學校裡最喜歡的科目是數學。許多人覺得數學很無聊、很困難,但我覺得它很有趣、很簡單。

　　為什麼我喜歡數學呢?在數學裡,你總是能夠知道答案是否正確。有些科目,像是英文或歷史,要知道答案是否正確有時很困難。

　　但對於數學,如果你找到一個答案,可以檢查看看它是否正確。如果它不正確,你可以一直做修改,直到找到正確答案為止。我喜歡數學的另一個原因是因為它是很有用的科目。如果你擅長數學,便可以做很多事情,找到許多好工作。

　　當我長大後,我想要當一個工程師,所以當我得找工作時,數學對我會非常有用。

# Example Answer 3

Of all my classes in school, I like economics the most. Economics is the study of economies and how money moves around in the world. Money is very important in our lives.

Some people think that money is the most important thing. So I think it is good to know all about money. Economics can be a difficult subject to study because there are many parts of economics that can be difficult to understand. But I still think it is very interesting.

My mother studied economics and now she has a very good job in a bank. She tells me that if I am really interested I should go to university to continue studying economics. I don't know what I'll want to do in the future, but right now, I'm most interested in economics.

## 範例解答三

在所有的學校科目中，我最喜歡經濟學。經濟學是研究經濟及世界上的金錢如何流通的學問。金錢在我們生活中非常重要。

有些人認為金錢是最重要的東西，所以我認為瞭解所有關於金錢的事是件好事。經濟學可以是很困難的科目，因為經濟學有許多部分，可能很難瞭解，但我還是很感興趣。

我媽媽以前是唸經濟學的，現在在銀行有份很好的工作。她告訴我，如果我真的對經濟學感興趣，我應該上大學，繼續攻讀經濟學。我不知道自己將來想做什麼，但是現在，我對經濟學最感興趣。

09

# Writing Question Number 3

### 寫作問題三

- Please use approximately 110 to 160 words to answer the question.

請使用大約110～160個字，來回答問題。

**Question** Do you think living in the country or in the city is better? Please explain and give reasons for your answer.

**問題** 你認為住在鄉下還是住在城市，哪一個比較好？請解釋為什麼，並提出理由。

文章開始 Start From Here

學 習 小 撇 步

## 把書讀進心坎裡

**讀聰明書，千萬不要死讀書！**

學習首重技巧，若能用對方法，自然而然能在各項考試中過關斬將，輕鬆拿高分。

以歷史科來說，很多人都覺得唸歷史是很煩人的事，要背一大堆莫名奇妙、跟自己一點關係都沒有的人名、事件、戰役等等，真的是浪費寶貴的青春歲月！不過，其實也沒那麼悲慘，換個角度想，學習也可以輕鬆自在。

要有效地獲得學習成果，讀書方法是很重要的。例如：在看書的同時，用圖表的方式將類似的歷史事件做歸納整理，常有令人意想不到的效果。也許你會說，這個東西不是參考書就有了嗎？不見得！畢竟自己整理的是最適合自己使用了。參考書裡的是很制式的邏輯整理，動手DIY，則任你天馬行空地用自己懂的方式來歸納，這比別人硬塞的東西更貼近自己的思考邏輯。而且因為是自己整理的，在整理的過程中，也加深了自己的記憶，可以不費吹灰之力地把歷史背下來。

所以，讀書可不能讀死書，呆呆地全盤接收。在閱讀的過程中，要適時地停下來思考，反芻一下剛剛閱讀的內容，如整理史地類的圖表，記下優美的、震撼人心的文學詞句等等。如此才能把書讀進心坎裡，書中的知識才能融入你的思想中，變成屬於你自己的東西。

Writing Answers　寫作問答

## Example Answer 1

I think that living in the city is better than living in the country. I am a young person and I like to do many things. I like going shopping, going to see movies and going to concerts. All of these things can only be done in a city.

If I lived in the country or a small town, I probably wouldn't be able to do many of these things. Also, most things are more convenient in a city. There are many busses, taxis, and subway stations so transportation is very convenient in a city.

But if I lived in the country, transportation would take more time and be less convenient. Maybe when I am older I will have a different opinion, but right now I feel that living in the city is best for me.

## 範例解答一

　　我認為住在城市比住在鄉下好。我是個年輕人，喜歡做許多事。我喜歡動物、看電影、聽音樂會。這些事只有在城裡才可以做到。

　　如果我住在鄉下或小鎮裡，這些事大概很多都做不成了。而且，在城市中，大部分的事都比較方便。城市裡有許多公車、計程車、地下鐵站，所以城市裡的交通很方便。

　　但如果我住在鄉下，交通會花上較多的時間，也沒有那麼方便。也許等我老一點時，我會有不同的看法，但現在我覺得住在城裡對我最好。

## Example Answer 2

I think that living in the country is the best place to live. For most of my life, I have lived in a small town. In a small town, people are friendlier than people in a city. In a city, most people are usually very busy and don't have time to be nice to each other.

But in the countryside, people are usually more relaxed, more friendly, and nicer to each other. One time, I went to live with my aunt in the city for a month. It was difficult to get used to. The traffic was noisy at night, the air was polluted, and I didn't like it very much.

At the end of the month, I was very happy to go back to my home in the country. I will go back to the city to visit my aunt someday, but I think I will always want to live in the country.

## 範例解答二

　　我認為鄉下是最適合居住的地方。我的大半生，都住在小鎮裡。小鎮裡的人們比城市的來的友善。在城市裡，大多數的人都非常忙碌，沒有時間對他人友善。

　　但在鄉下，人們通常比較悠閒、較為友善、對他人較親切。有一次，我到城裡去和阿姨住了一個月，很難習慣那裡的生活。晚上交通很吵，空氣污染，我不是很喜歡。

　　那個月結束後，我很高興回到鄉下的家。有一天我會回到城市去探望我阿姨，但我想我會永遠想住在鄉下。

Part 2

Writing Answers

寫作問答

## Example Answer 3

Living in the city and living in the country both have their advantages. In the city, there are more things to do in your free time, but in the country, life can be more relaxing.

I think it is better to live in the country when you are young. Children can have more fun growing up in the country than in the city. In the country, children can go outside and play in lakes and fields and mountains. They couldn't do these things if they lived in the city.

But for adults it might be better to live in a city. There are more jobs in the city than in the country, and it is very important for adults to have good jobs.

Also, jobs in the city usually pay more money than jobs in the country. So I think people always have the choice between living in the city or living in the country, and they should choose which is best for them.

## 範例解答三

　　住在城市和鄉下各有各的優點。在城市裡，人們在空閒時，有比較多的事情可以做。但在鄉下，生活可能比較悠閒。

　　我認為一個人小時候最好住在鄉下。孩童在鄉下成長，過得會比在城裡快樂。在鄉下，孩子們可以到外面玩，在湖泊、田野和山裡面玩。如果住在城裡，他們便不能做這些事。

　　但對成人來說，住在城裡可能比較好。城市裡的工作機會比鄉下多，對成人來說，有份好工作是很重要的。

　　再者，與鄉下相比，城裡的工作薪水比較高。所以我想人們可以在鄉下和城市中做選擇，選出對他們最有利的居住環境。

# Writing　Question　Number　4

## 寫作問題四

- Please use approximately 110 to 160 words to answer the question.
  請使用大約110～160個字，來回答問題。

Question Do you think it is important for people to learn a second language? What are the advantages of knowing a second language?

問題　你認為學習第二外語對人們是否重要？會說第二外語有什麼好處？

文章開始　Start From Here

## 學習小撇步

### 多動腦，勤提筆

**廣泛閱讀各類文章，是培養寫作能力必下的工夫！**

不過，一般人常常只「讀」不「寫」，殊不知平常若不勤提筆寫文章，就算飽覽詩書，臨場應試，還是寫不出流暢文章的。

我們能藉著閱讀，增加字彙，以及學習各種中文的英文表達法，也能效法他人文章起承轉合的技巧。但對於文章的鋪陳、邏輯能力，卻是得靠平常練習來累積的。一個人的字彙量再多，寫出來的文句再優美，若沒有完整的架構，勉強拼湊起，還是會顯得毫無章法，這樣的文章，充其量只是文字的堆砌！

文章要傑出，別無他法，一定要勤動筆，這樣才能發現自己寫作的盲點，再藉由閱讀大量相關文章來彌補缺失。

若對於寫作能力較無信心者，不妨先選定閱讀一篇文章後，再模擬其寫作方式、用字，寫出類似的文章。之後，再慢慢發展自己的主題，寫出真正屬於自己的文章。

若欲培養寫作邏輯能力，可利用模擬連鎖式題目，來練習寫作。如「我今天上學遲到」，這句話可發展出如「為什麼遲到」、「遲到後是否發生什麼事」，接下來就針對以上問題的答案再發展出不同主題，如此不斷發展，可以激盪你的腦力，培養你對文章發展合理性的敏感度，讓你徹底掌握文句的連貫性。只要把握以上建議，加以練習，相信往後面對各類寫作題目，都能下筆有如神助，寫作成績傲視群雄。

Writing Answers　寫作問答

## Example Answer 1

I think it is very important for people to learn a second language.

In our modern world, we often have to communicate with people from different countries. Sometimes, this can be very difficult. Sometimes, it's even impossible. This is why it's important for everyone to know how to speak a second language.

Many people say that English is the global language. This means that around the globe people can use English to communicate with each other.

Also, English is very important for people in business. If you go into any big company anywhere in the world, chances are you'll be able to find someone who can speak English.

So I think it is very important for people to know a second language, and in many cases English is one of the most useful languages to know.

## 範例解答一

我認為學習第二語言對人們非常重要。

在現在的世界上，我們常常需要和來自不同國家的人們溝通。有時這是很困難的，有時甚至是不可能的。這就是為什麼每個人都必須要會說第二外語。

許多人說英語是國際語言，這表示全世界的人能夠使用英語和彼此溝通。

同時，英語對商業界的人來說非常重要。如果你進入世界上任何一家大公司，你一定能找到會說英文的人。

所以我認為會說第二語言是非常重要的，而在許多情況中，英文是最有用的語言之一。

# Example Answer 2

I think it is important for some people to learn a second language. But I don't think it is necessary for everyone to learn a second language.

For example, if you are a person who travels to other countries, then it's important for you to learn a second language. If you only know one language and you travel to a foreign country, then there's a chance the people there won't be able to understand you.

Secondly, if you're a person who has to do business with the foreigners, then it will be helpful if you can speak their language. But I don't think every person needs to learn a second language. For example, if you always live in the same place and everyone there speaks the same language, then there's no need for you to learn a second language.

In conclusion, I would say that the need to learn a second language depends on the person and their circumstances.

## 範例解答二

　　我認為學第二外語對某些人是非常重要的，但我不認為每一個人都應該這樣做。

　　例如，如果你是一個常常旅行到他國的人，那你有必要學習第二外語。如果你只會一種語言，然後又到他國旅行，就有可能碰到那裡的人不瞭解你想要說些什麼的時候了。

　　再者，如果你必須和外國人做生意，而你會說他們的語言的話，那會很有幫助的。但我不認為每個人都需要學習第二外語。舉例來說，如果你總是住在同一個地方，而那裡的每個人都說同一種語言，那你就沒有必要學習第二種語言。

　　總結說來，學習第二外語的必要與否，端視個人及他們的處境而定。

# Example Answer 3

I think that knowing a second language is essential for any person who likes to travel. I'd like to use an example from my own life to prove this point.

Two years ago, I went to Canada with my family. My mother and father cannot speak English, but my sister and I can. One day, we were walking around the city of Vancouver. My mother and father wanted to go see a museum, but we didn't know where it was. My sister had an idea. She suggested that we ask someone on the street where the museum was. So she and I went to ask a woman where the museum was. The woman was very nice and helpful and showed us on the map. Then, my family went to the museum and we had a great day.

This would not have been possible if my sister and I couldn't speak a second language.

## 範例解答三

　　我認為每個喜歡旅行的人，都有必要會説第二種語言。我想要用自己生活中的例子來舉證。

　　兩年前，我和家人去加拿大玩。我父母不會説英文，但我和姊姊會。有一天，我們在溫哥華市區逛，我父母想要去參觀博物館，但我們不知道怎麼走。於是我姊姊出了個主意，她建議我們在街上找個路人來問博物館的地點。所以我們兩個人問了一個婦人，有關博物館的地點。她人很好，樂於助人，並在地圖上指出博物館的位置。後來，我們一家人去了博物館，過了很愉快的一天。

　　如果姊姊和我都不會説第二外語的話，這一切都不可能發生。

# Writing Question Number 5

## 寫作問題五

- Please use approximately 110 to 160 words to answer the question.

  請使用大約110～160個字，來回答問題。

**Question** A vegetarian is a person who does not eat meat. Some people say that it's more healthy not to eat meat, but other people say that eating meat is important for people. What do you think?

**問題** 素食者不吃肉，有些人說不吃肉比較健康，但也有人說肉類對人體很重要，你覺得呢？

文章開始 Start From Here

# Learning Skills

## 學 習 小 撇 步

## 掌握學習小技巧‧英語能力迅速提升

其實，學英文就跟學中文一樣。無論學任何一種語言，方法都是可以套用的。找出適合自己的學習方法並不難，只要發揮創意，把自己平常習慣的學習模式套用上去，就不會太勉強，也可以輕鬆自然的學好英文。這些小技巧包括：

1. **心情小札記**：隨身帶一本小札記。就像寫日記一樣，用英文跟自己對話，不會寫的就先用中文代替，隨後再查字典補充上去。這樣的方法，有下列好處：

   （1）由於語言的隔閡，可免去直接被窺探的可能 。

   （2）幫自己訂做一個潘朵拉的盒子（永遠有「希望」（Hope）」，裡面裝滿了英文的小秘密。

   （3）寫錯了不怕別人笑，輕鬆又無負擔。久而久之，英文功力增強於無形之中。

2. **用英文寫信**：上網結交世界各地的筆友，約定用英文溝通，交換彼此的生活經驗及想法。網路的普及，讓身為 e 世代的英語學習者，的確是佔了一些優勢！

3. **多閱讀**：閱讀是累積「字彙」財產的必要程序，有了豐富的字彙量，才能由字成句，句再成文，逐漸累積寫作功力。

4. **結合興趣**：人對於自己喜愛的事物，總會有著一股衝勁與狂熱，在接觸這些資訊的同時，不妨也多多參考外文版本，世界無奇不有，往往會因為好奇心的驅使，而在更寬廣的世界中受益無窮。

   總之，找出最適合自己的學習方式，學習就能輕鬆、有趣又得意！

## Example Answer 1

I think being a vegetarian is a good thing.

In our modern world, meat has become very cheap and very available. For these reasons, many people eat meat. Actually, many people eat too much meat. And this can be very unhealthy.

We know that meat contains a lot of fat, and too much fat is not good for our bodies. We also know that vegetables contain many important vitamins. Scientists have shown that people who eat more vegetables live longer and healthier lives.

So, although it may be very difficult for people to stop eating meat, I think it is a good decision and will make a person much healthier.

## 範例解答一

我覺得吃素是件好事。

在現今的世界中，肉類變得非常廉價、到處都是，因此，許多人都吃肉。事實上，許多人吃太多肉了，這是非常不健康的。我們都知道肉類含有許多脂肪，而太多脂肪對身體不好。

我們也知道蔬菜含有許多重要的維他命。科學家證明多吃蔬菜的人，活得較長、較健康。

所以雖然可能很難叫人們停止吃肉，我仍覺得這是一個好決定，也會使人更健康。

## Example Answer 2

I don't think it's a good idea for people to only eat vegetables.

Human bodies are designed to eat both meat and vegetables. If we look at the history of humans, we can see that humans have always eaten both meat and vegetables.

I think this tells us that humans must eat both meat and vegetables in order to stay healthy. So if a person decides to stop eating meat, then there is a chance that person would become sick. Of course, a person cannot eat only meat and no vegetables because this too would be unhealthy.

So I think that it's best for people to eat a good combination of meat and vegetables. This is the best way for people to stay healthy and live for a long time.

## 範例解答二

我不認為只吃蔬菜是件好事。

人體的設計，需要吃肉類及蔬菜。如果我們看看人類歷史，就可知道人類長久以來一直是肉和蔬菜都吃。

這告訴我們人類必須要肉和蔬菜都吃，才能維持健康。所以如果一個人決定不再吃肉，他就有可能會生病。當然，人也不能光吃肉，不吃蔬菜，因為這也很不健康。

所以我認為人類最好是兩者均衡食用，這是讓人們維持健康、長壽的最好方式。

## Example Answer 3

I am not a vegetarian but I think it's good that some people eat only vegetables.

Vegetables are much easier to grow and the world could feed more people if everyone only ate vegetables. So I think that if more people were vegetarians, then there would be fewer hungry people in the world.

But there is another problem to consider. There are many farmers in the world who have cows, pigs, and chickens. These farmers need people to buy their meat in order to earn money. If everyone stopped eating meat, then these farmers would lose their jobs. And this would be very bad too.

So I think this is a difficult question and there is no simple answer.

## 範例解答三

我不是素食者，但我認為有些人只吃蔬菜是件好事。

蔬菜比較容易種植，且如果人們都只吃蔬菜的話，這個世界就可以提供更多人食物。所以我認為如果更多人吃素，世界上就不會有這麼多人挨餓。

但我們要思考一個問題，世界上有許多農夫，畜養牛、豬及雞，他們需要人們 買他們的肉品才能賺錢。如果人們都停止吃肉，那這些農夫就會失去工作，這也非常不好。

所以我認為這個問題很困難，沒有簡單的解答。

# Writing Question Number 6

### 寫作問題六

- Please use approximately 110 to 160 words to answer the question.

請使用大約110～160個字，來回答問題。

**Question** If you could choose any animal in the world to be your pet, which animal would you choose? Why would you choose this animal?

**問題** 如果你可以選擇世界上任何一種動物，當作寵物，你會選哪一種？為什麼呢？

文章開始　Start From Here

## Learning Skills 學 習 小 撇 步

### 跟上時代的腳步，在網路世界尋寶

　　現代網路科技發達，各類千奇百怪的資訊在網路上都可搜尋的到。只要善用網路資源，各種教導寫作的英文網站，都是很值得參考的。因為這些網站大都是由以英語為母語的人士所設立的，可以從中學到道地英文寫作的技巧，如標點符號的使用方式、引用他人文章該注意的事項等等，這是訓練自己的寫作方向符合標準英文寫作的最佳管道之一。

　　網路的另一項好處是方便省時。當我們想寫某一類型的文章時，只要在網路上查詢，便有成千上百篇的文章供我們參考。且現在的考試題型多以時事為趨勢，在網路上，可以迅速搜尋到各種最新最流行的資訊，除了傳統寫作主題外，還可隨時掌握最熱門話題的英語表達法，做好萬全準備，考試就不怕無從發揮起了。現在就身體力行，趕快上網去挖寶吧！

## Example Answer 1

If I could choose any animal to have as a pet I would choose a tiger.

Some people may think I'm crazy to want such a dangerous animal. But I don't think tigers are that dangerous.

If you get a tiger when it's very young and small, then you can train it. You can train it to be nice to people, you can train it to do tricks, and you can also train it not to hurt people. Of course having a tiger could be dangerous, but I think if you are very careful and you know a lot about the animal, then you will be safe.

Also, there are not many tigers left in the wild. If I could have a tiger as a pet, then I would protect it and make sure that it had a long and healthy life.

## 範例解答一

　　如果我可以選擇任何一種動物當寵物，我會選擇老虎。

　　有些人也許會認為我瘋了，才會想要這麼危險的物，但我不認為老虎有那麼危險。

　　如果你買一隻幼虎，你就可以訓練牠。你可以訓練牠對人們友善，你可以訓練牠去玩一些把戲，你也可以訓練牠不要傷害人們。當然，養一隻老虎可能會很危險，但我覺得如果一個人很小心，並且非常瞭解這種動物，那他應該會很安全。

　　再者，世界上的野生老虎所剩不多，如果我可以養一隻老虎當寵物，我就可以保護牠，確保牠長壽、健康。

## Example Answer 2

If I could have any animal as a pet, I would like to have a dolphin.

Dolphins are one of the smartest animals in the world. Many people think that dolphins are fish, but they are not. Dolphins are actually mammals. They come from the same family of animals as people.

In fact, dolphins do many things that people do. Dolphins play in the water just for fun. Dolphins live together with their families and help protect each other.

But there's just one problem. Dolphins live in the ocean and they need a lot of water to live. So I think it would be very difficult to have a dolphin as a pet.

## 範例解答二

如果我可以選擇任何動物當寵物，我會選擇海豚。

海豚是世界上最聰明的動物之一。許多人認為海豚是魚類，但事實上並不是。海豚其實是哺乳類，和人類是同一族類。

實際上，海豚會做許多人類會做的事。海豚在海裡嬉戲只是因為好玩，牠們和家人住在一起，彼此互相保護。

但只有一個問題，海豚住在海裡，牠們需要很多水才能存活，所以我認為要養海豚當寵物是件很困難的事。

Writing Answers

寫作問答

## Example Answer 3

My favorite animal in the whole world is the eagle. So if I could choose any animal for a pet, I would definitely choose an eagle.

Why do I like eagles?

First, I think eagles are one of the most beautiful animals on the planet. Second, I think it would be very fun to watch my eagle fly around. Third, if I had an eagle as a pet, all of my friends would like to come see it and this would make me very popular.

Of course, having an eagle as a pet would not be easy. Eagles can fly very high, very fast and very far. So if I had an eagle as a pet, I would always worry that it would fly away and not come back.

# 範例解答三

　　世界上我最喜歡的動物是老鷹，所以如果我可以選任何一種動物當寵物，我絕對會選擇老鷹。

　　為什麼呢？

　　第一，我認為老鷹是地球上最美麗的動物之一。第二，我認為看我的老鷹四處遨翔，應該會很好玩。第三，如果我養一隻老鷹當寵物，我所有的朋友都會想來看看牠，這會讓我變得很受歡迎。

　　當然，養一隻老鷹當寵物並不簡單。老鷹可以飛的很高、很快、很遠，所以如果我養一隻老鷹當寵物，我會一直擔心，牠會不會飛走，就不回來了。

- What is worth doing is worth doing well.
  （凡是值得做的事，就值得好好的去做。）

- Think before you act.
  （三思而後行。）

- Think today and speak tomorrow.
  （今天先想好，明天再說出口。）

- Practice what you preach.
  （言出必行。）

- The work praises the man.
  （工作肯定人的價值。）

# Writing Corrections
## 寫作改正

## Instructions

This part of the book will help you practice correcting mistakes. As we said at the start of the book: after you write, you will also need to edit your composition. So take a look at these essays and see if you can correct the mistakes.

寫作指示

　　本書這部分將幫助你練習如何改正錯誤。如同本書一開始提及的，在你寫作後，你會需要編審自己的作文，所以看看下列這些文章，你知道如何改正錯誤嗎？

# Writing Correction Number 1

 寫作改正一

**Instructions** Read the following passages, try to find mistakes and correct them.
閱讀下列文章，改正錯誤並在右側空格內作答。

　　Next summer, I will take a vakation with my family, but we are still try to decide where we should went. My mother said she wants to go to canada, but my father want to go to Mexico. My sister and me don't really care where we go, as long as we can go somewhere.

明年夏天，我將會和家人一起去度假，但我們還在苦思要去哪裡玩。我媽說她想要去加拿大，但我爸想要去墨西哥。姊姊和我不在乎要去哪裡，只要可以去哪裡玩玩就好。

My mother like the idea of go to Canada for several reasons. Her said it is very safe and clean there. Also she said that we could go in Quebec, which is the French part of Canada. There it could practice speaking French eat French food, and feel like we had left North America. but my father doesn't know how to speak French. Also, my dad thinks that Canada is really no differ from the United States, so go there would not be that specialty.

> 我媽媽想去加拿大，有好幾個原因。她說那裡很安全、乾淨。她也說我們可以去魁北克，那是加拿大的法語區。在那裡，她可以練習說法語、吃法國食物、體會一下離開北美的感覺，但我爸爸不會說法語。而且他認為加拿大和美國真的沒有什麼不同，所以去那裡也沒有什麼特別。

My dad say that going to Mexico would be more fun then going to Canada. He says Mexico is a Country that's very different for the U.S. or Canada. In Mexico, they spoke Spanish. Actually, they speak Mexican, but that very similar to Spanish. My dad also love Mexican food, and so do my sister and I. But my mom think that Mexico is unsafe and also unclean, so she says in would be a bad place to go.

爸爸說去墨西哥會比去加拿大好玩，他說墨西哥是個非常不同於美國與加拿大的國家。在墨西哥，人們說西班牙語。實際上，他們說墨西哥語，那和西語非常相似。爸爸也喜愛墨西哥食物，姊姊和我也是如此。但媽媽認為墨西哥不安全、也不乾淨。所以她說最好不要去那裡。

So right now we are still try to decide where we are go next summer. My mom really wants we to go to Canada, and my dad thinks going to Mexico would be beter. I guess we will probably just having to wait and see. But like I saying before, my sister and I would become happy to go anywhere.

所以現在我們仍在想明年夏天要去哪裡。媽媽真的很想去加拿大，但爸爸認為去墨西哥比較好，我猜我們大概要等著看了。但就像我之前說過的，姊姊和我去哪裡都會很高興。

## 解析　**The Corrected Article**

Next summer, I will take a **vacation❶** with my family, but we are still **trying❷** to decide where we should **go❸**. My mother said she wants to go to **Canada❹**, but my father **wants❺** to go to Mexico. My sister and I**❻** don't really care where we go, as long as we can go somewhere.

My mother **likes❼** the idea of **going❽** to Canada for several reasons. **She❾** said it is very safe and clean there. Also she said that we could go **to❿** Quebec, which is the French part of Canada. There **we⓫** could practice speaking French,**⓬** eat French food, and feel like we had left North America. **But⓭** my father doesn't know how to speak French.

Part **3**

寫作改正 Writing Corrections

Also, my dad thinks that Canada is really no **different⑭** from the United States, so **going⑮** there would not be that **special⑯**.

My dad **said⑰** that going to Mexico would be more fun **than⑱** going to Canada. He says Mexico is a **country⑲** that's very different **from⑳** the U.S. or Canada. In Mexico, they **speak㉑** Spanish. Actually, they speak Mexican, but **that's㉒** very similar to Spanish. My dad also **loves㉓** Mexican food, and so do my sister and I. But my mom **thinks㉔** that Mexico is unsafe and also unclean, so she says **it㉕** would be a bad place to go.

So right now we are still **trying㉖** to decide where we **will㉗** go next summer. My mom really wants **us㉘** to go to Canada, and my dad thinks going to Mexico would be **better㉙**. I guess we will probably just **have㉚** to wait and see. But like I **said㉛** before, my sister and I would **be㉜** happy to go anywhere.

Writing Corrections

寫作改正

## 解析　**Explanations**

**❶ vakation→vacation**

這個字的正確拼法是vacation。

**❷ try→trying**

動詞時態錯誤。你可以從主要動詞為are判斷，這句話是現在式。所以try應該改成現在進行式trying。

**❸ went→go**

動詞時態錯誤，正確答案是go。

**❹ canada→Canada**

專有名詞如人名、地名，第一個字母要大寫，故改成Canada。

**❺ want→wants**

主詞動詞一致。記住，動詞字尾的變化隨主詞而定。在這個句子中，主詞是father（父親），所以詞應該加上s，改為wants。

**❻ me→I**

代名詞錯誤。me這個字為受詞，此處應該改成I。

學生常常搞錯me和I的用法，有個簡單的方法可以知道該用me還是I，就是拿掉另一個主詞，然後分別用me和I套入句子中，看看哪個比較適合。舉例來說，在 "My sister and（me/I）don't really care where we go" 中，我們可以把 "My sister and" 拿掉，然後只剩下 "(I/me) don't really care where to go" 的部分，看到這個簡化的句子，很明顯的，應該用I。

### ❼ like→likes

主詞動詞一致。主詞為第三人稱，動詞就必須隨之變化，因此這個句子的動詞應從like改為likes。

### ❽ go→going

介係詞＋名詞/ V-ing，故go應改為going。

### ❾ Her→She

代名詞錯誤，her 為所有格，不能單獨做主詞，這裡應該用She。

### ❿ in→to

這裡應該用to。記住，在英文中，去某處的介係詞都用 to。

Part 3

Writing Corrections

寫作改正

129

**⓫ it→we**

代名詞錯誤。因為這個故事的主詞是家庭family，應把it改為we。整個句子應為There we could practice speaking French.。

**⓬ speaking French eat French food, and...　→speaking French, eat French food, and feel like we had left North America.**

少標點符號。在列舉時，須用逗點來分隔片語或物件，應把句子改成：There we could practice speaking French, eat French food, and feel like we had left North America.

**⓭ but→But**

改成But，句子開頭第一個字母一定要大寫。

**⓮ differ→different**

詞性錯誤。differ 這個字是動詞，但在這個句子裡應該要用形容詞different。

**⓯ go→going**

錯誤動詞變化。這裡應該要用現在進行式，所以go要改成going。

**⑯ specialty→special**

詞性錯誤。specialty 這個字是名詞，但這個句子應該要用形容詞 special。

**⑰ say→said**

動詞時態錯誤。這裡應該要用過去式，因為父親已經說過這句話了，所以say要改成過去式said。

**⑱ then→than**

用字錯誤。這個句子中，父親在比較兩件事，在比較時，要用than這個字，而不是then。舉例來說，「冰比水要來得冷」是：Ice is colder than water。then是指「然後」之意。

**⑲ Country→country**

這個字不應該以大寫開頭。只有國家名稱之類的專有名詞，才以大寫開頭，像是Japan（日本）、Australia（澳洲）、France（法國）等。

**⑳ for→from**

這裡的for應該改成from，表示「A不同於B」的正確句型為：A is different from B。

Part **3**

Writing Corrections

寫作改正

**㉑ spoke→speak**

動詞時態錯誤。這個動詞不該用過去式,因為「在墨西哥的人們說西班牙語」這個句子是陳述一個事實,所以應該用現在式speak。

**㉒ that→that's或that is**

這個句子裡缺少動詞。必須補上動詞is,將that改為that's或that is,才是個完整正確的句子。

**㉓ love→loves**

動詞變化。記住,動詞和主詞必須一致。這句的主詞是My dad(我爸爸),第三人稱單數,love這個字必須加上s。

**㉔ think→thinks**

動詞變化錯誤。動詞必須與主詞一致。這個句子應改為But my mom thinks...。

**㉕ in→it**

這裡的in應改為it,因為它指的是墨西哥這個地點。

**㉖ try→trying**

動詞時態錯誤。這個句子應該是現在進行式,所以詞應該是trying,而不是try。

**㉗ are→will**

動詞時態錯誤。這句應該用未來式，因為指的是明年夏天。這個句子應改為：So right now, we are still trying to decide where we will go next summer.。記住，will這個字，是用來表示未來式。

**㉘ we→us**

代名詞錯誤。因為「我們」的動詞的受格，是us這個字，看看下面這個例子：He likes us. We like him.。we應用做主格，受格應用us。

**㉙ beter→better**

拼字錯誤。這個字的正確拼法是better。

**㉚ having→have**

動詞時態錯誤。這裡應用原形動詞have。

**㉛ saying→said**

動詞時態錯誤。這個句子用了before這個字，可判斷出這是過去式。故這個句子的動詞應該用過去式said。

**㉜ become→be**

用字錯誤。這裡應該用be這個字。

# Writing Correction Number 2

## Part 1

## 寫作改正二

### 第一部份

What do you think around cell phones? When I first got one three and four years ago, I thought it is great. I could call my friends from anytime and have a chat. If I was lost, I can call someone and ask for direcsions. If me was going to be late for a meet, I could call the person and let him know. Or if I was just boring and had nothing to do, than I could call a friend just to say hello.

你對手機有何看法？當我三、四年前擁有第一支手機時，我覺得它棒極了。我可以在任何地方打電話跟朋友聊天。如果我迷路了，我可以打電話向某人問路。如果我約會快要遲到了，我可以打電話告知對方。或是如果我很無聊，沒事可做，我就可以打電話跟朋友問好。

But slowly, my cell phone starting to annoy me. The bigger problem was that it would ring at unconvenient times. Four example, one time I am on the bus. My hands were full of shopping bag and I was tried to find some change in my pocket to pay the bus fair. So, to summarize the situation, my hands were full and me was quite busy.

　　但逐漸地，我的手機開始困擾我。最大的問題是，它會在不適當的時間響起。舉例來說，有一次，我在公車上，我手上提滿購物袋，我試著在口袋裡找些零錢付車資。長話短說，我手上都是東西，忙碌不已。

## 解析　The Corrected Article

What do you think **about①** cell phones? When I first got one three **or②** four years ago, I thought it **was③** great. I could call my friends from **anywhere④** and have a chat. If I was lost, I **could⑤** call someone and ask for **directions⑥**. If **I⑦** was going to be late for a **meeting⑧**, I could call the person and let him know. Or if I was just **bored⑨** and had nothing to do, **then⑩** I could call a friend just to say hello.

But slowly, my cell phone **started⑪** to annoy me. The **biggest⑫** problem was that it would ring at **inconvenient⑬** times.

For⑭ example, one time I **was**⑮ on the bus. My hands were full of shopping **bags**⑯ and I was **trying**⑰ to find some change in my pocket to pay the bus **fare**⑱. So, to summarize the situation, my hands were full and I⑲ was quite busy.

## 解析　Explanations

### ❶ around→about

介係詞錯誤。應該要用about這個字。英文中常用這一類的用語，像是What do you think about the weather?（你覺得天氣如何？)或是What do you think about Lisa?（你覺得麗莎怎麼樣？）

### ❷ and→or

這裡應該要用or這個字。這位作者正在估算，他大概是在什麼時候得到第一支手機。句子應該是：When I first got one three or four years ago, I thought...。這個人不能確定那到底是三年前或四年前的事，所以應用or。

### ❸ is→was

動詞時態錯誤。注意這個句子由過去式開頭，When I first got...。got這個動詞是過去式，所以is這個字應改為was。

### ❹ anytime→anywhere

地方副詞錯誤。這個字應改為anywhere。注意，這個副詞前用了from這個介係詞，通常from這個字接

Part 3

Writing Corrections

寫作改正

的是一個地方。看看以下兩個例子：I come from England.（我來自英國）；She walked here from downtown.（她從市中心走到這裡）。

### ❺ can→could

動詞時態錯誤。這個句子由過去式開始，因為動詞是was。所以這裡要用正確的動詞時態could，如：If I was lost, I could call someone and ask...。

### ❻ direcsions→directions

拼字錯誤。許多英文字的結尾是tion或sion，但tion結尾比較普遍。在讀到新的字彙時，要注意這點。這個字的正確拼法是direction。

### ❼ me→I

錯誤代名詞。me為受詞，但卻用在這個句子的主詞位置上，所以應用代名詞"I"來當做主詞。注意，這兩個字的用法，端看句子需要的是主詞或受詞。看看下面的例子：I think she likes me.（我想她喜歡我）或I want you to talk to me.（我要你和我說話）。如果是句子的主詞就用"I"，如果是受詞就用"me"。

**⑧ meet→meeting**

用字錯誤。for後面要接名詞，meet常做動詞，而meeting是名詞，故需改為meeting。看看下面這個例子：I will meet you in the meeting.（我會在會議中和你見面）。

**⑨ boring→bored**

用字錯誤。正確的字是bored。boring這個字是用來描述某件事很無趣或不好玩，而bored這個字描述某人在做某事時，感到很無聊的一種感覺。看看下面這些例子：The children were bored because the game was boring.（因為遊戲不好玩，所以孩子們感到很無聊）或 I felt very bored watching that boring movie.（看那部無聊的電影讓我感到很無趣）。通常我們不會在同一個句子中，同時使用這兩個字。這裡只是舉例，讓大家分辨它們的不同之處。

**⑩ than→then**

用字錯誤。than這個字應改為then。If...then...這個句型在英文中很常見。看看下面這些例子：If I don't drive faster, then I'll be late for work.（如果我不開快一點，上班就會遲到）或是If it rains

Part 3

Writing Corrections

寫作改正

tomorrow, then we won't go to the park.（如果明天下雨，我們就不去公園）。

**⑪ starting→started**

動詞時態錯誤。記住，這整篇作文是用過去式寫成，因此正確的動詞是started。

**⑫ bigger→biggest**

形容詞錯誤。bigger是形容詞比較級，只用在兩件或多件事物的比較上。在這個句子中，應用big或biggest，才是正確的。

**⑬ unconvenient→inconvenient**

字首錯誤。convenient 的反義字是 inconvenient。注意un-和in-這兩個字首，都是表「相反、否定」之意，但用在不同的字上，需特別注意，不要混淆了。

**⑭ Four→For**

拼字錯誤。這個句子中，作者不是要說四（four），而是要說for example，這是英文中常見的片語。

**⑮ am→was**

動詞時態錯誤。再次提醒你，這篇作文是用過去式寫成，正確的動詞是was。當學生寫英文作文時，常

常會用錯時態。要牢記，寫完作文後，要再次檢查，時態是否完全一致。

### ⑯ bag→bags

應該用複數bags。仔細看看這個句子：My hands were full of shopping bag. 如果你的手拿滿某物，這代表不只是一樣東西。所以這個句子，應該要用複數bags。

### ⑰ tried→trying

動詞時態錯誤，這個字應改成 trying。你或許會認為這篇文章是以過去式寫成，所以全部的動詞都應用過去式，但英文的文法規則可不是這麼簡單。因為過去動詞 was 在 try 之前，所以 try 這個字必須加 ing，表示過去進行式。

### ⑱ fair→fare

用字錯誤。別因為有些英文字聽起來一樣，拼法不同而被搞混了。這裡要用的字是 fare，它的意思是做某事「所需付出的金錢」，像是搭公車要付的車資。

### ⑲ me→I

錯誤代名詞。記住我們之前提過的一個重要原則：如果是句子的主詞便使用代名詞"I"這個字，如果當句子的受詞，便用 me 這個字。在這個句子中，其角色是主詞，所以要用"I"這個字。這是許多學生常犯的錯誤，你應該要練習這兩個字的用法，直到能運用自如為止。

Part **3**

Writing Corrections

寫作改正

143

## Instructions

Okay, now you are on your own. The following part has twelve mistakes. But they are not underlined. See if you can find and correct the mistakes on your own before looking at the answers. Good luck!

寫作指示

　　好了，現在你要靠自己了。以下這部分有十二個錯誤，但並沒有用底線標出來，試試看你能否找出錯誤，並自行將其更正，之後再對對看答案。祝你好運！

# Writing Correction Number 2

## Part 2

寫作改正二

第二部份

What happening next? You guessed it, my cell phone rang, at first, I pretended I didn't hear them. Then person on the bus started looking at me. They were thinking, "Why doesn't he answer his phone." As I reached down to answer my phone I dropped the change for bus fare that is in my hand. The change hit the floor and rolled away. Then as I tried to lift the phone to me ear, one of the shopping bags in my hand hit a little girl on the head! She started screamed and cried. I felt so bad.

接下來發生了什麼事呢？你猜猜看，我的手機響了。起初，我假裝沒有聽到鈴聲。然後公車上的人開始盯著我看。他們在想「為什麼這個人不接電話呢？」正當我伸手去接電話時，我手上拿來要付車資的零錢掉了出來。零錢掉到地上，滾得好遠。然後當我試著把電話放到耳邊時，我手中的一個動物袋打到一個小女孩的頭。她開始尖叫、大哭，我感覺糟透了。

Final, I answered my phone. Do you know what the person who called said? They said, "Hi. I'd like three cheeseburgers, two orders of French fries, and two cokes delivered to my house at number 144 main street."

最後，我接起了電話。你知道打電話來的人說了些什麼嗎？他說：「嗨，我想點三個起士漢堡、兩份薯條、兩杯可樂，送到我家，地址是緬因街一四四號。」

"What?" I said, "You must have dialed the wrong number!" I was very angrily that this person had interrupted me when I was so busy. So although cell phones can be very convenient, it can also be equally inconvenient. And sometimes I think life would be easier if cell phones were never invented.

　　我說：「什麼？你一定是撥錯號碼了。」這個人在我這麼忙碌的時候打擾我，讓我實在很生氣。因此雖然手機很便利，相同地，也有其不便利。有時我會想：如果從來沒有發明過手機的話，生活就會簡單許多。

## 解析   The Corrected Article

What **happened①** next? You guessed it, my cell phone rang. **At②** first, I pretended that I didn't hear **it③**. Then **people④** on the bus started looking at me. They were thinking, "Why doesn't he answer his phone?"**⑤** As I reached down to answer my phone I dropped the change for bus fare that **was⑥** in my hand. The change hit the floor and rolled away. Then as I tried to lift the phone to my ear, one of the shopping bags in my hand hit a little girl on the head! She started **screaming and crying⑦**. I felt so bad.

Finally**⑧**, I answered my phone. Do you know what the person who called said? **He❾** said, "Hi. I'd like three cheeseburgers, two orders of French fries, and two cokes delivered to my house at number 144 **Main Street❿**."

"What?" I said, "You must have dialed the wrong number!" I was very **angry⓫** that this person had interrupted me when I was so busy. So although cell phones can be very convenient, **they⓬** can also be equally inconvenient. And sometimes I think life would be easier if cell phones were never invented.

## 解析　**Explanations**

**❶ happening→happened**

改成過去式happened。

**❷ ...rang, at first...→...rang. At first...**

at first屬於另一個句子，故應改成...rang. At first...。

**❸ them→it**

這邊的受詞代表的是「電話鈴響」這件事，是單數，故要改成it。

**❹ person→people**

「公車上的人」不止一個，故person要用複數people。

**❺ Why doesn't he answer his phone.**
**　→Why doesn't he answer his phone?**

這句是疑問句，句尾要用問號？。

**❻ is→was**

要改成was。

**❼ screamed and cried→screaming and crying**

start + to V/Ving，故要改成 screaming and crying。

**❽ Final→Finally**

這邊應用副詞Finally（終於，最後）。

**❾ They→He**

這邊的主詞是指 "the person"，為單數，故應改為 He。

**❿ main street→Main Street**

這是街道名稱，屬於專有名詞，故要改成Main Street。

**⓫ angrily→angry**

表示某人感到生氣，要用形容詞 angry。

**⓬ it→they**

這邊主詞是cell phones，代名詞要用複數they。

- Time and industry produce every day new knowledge.

  （時間與勤勞，使學識與日俱增。）

- A young idler, an old beggar.

  （少壯不努力，老大徒傷悲。）

- If you want knowledge, you must toil for it.

  （想求知，要能知苦。）

- By doing nothing we learn to do ill.

  （無所事事，學會行惡。）

- An investment in education pays the best dividends.

  （投資教育獲利最大。）

# Part

4

Appendix 附錄

這句英文，改變你的人生

## 1

# Live and learn.
## 活到老學到老。

### 故事分享

　　TVBS董事長董事長張孝威曾說：「以人類的智慧，能找到的答案還是有限，即使已經翻遍了每一顆石頭找答案，還是要停下來想想，從更高的層次來看，自己究竟處在什麼位置上。」

　　有許多人都是在退休之後才頓感虛空，成天看著快被翻爛的報紙，整天拿著電視的遙控器，不斷的轉台，找不到寂寞的出口。直到報名了大學的進修課程之後，才終於找到了宣洩管道，開始當起了有目標的「老學生」。

　　老學生的現象，顯示出學習的魅力，也顯示出學習是不分年齡的。不論何種年齡的人，都可以開心的學習，不管是聽課、做作業、交朋友，在學習的面前，每個人都變得無比的平等，單純、又滿足。

有一家連鎖的日語學習班，在開學招新生時，來了一個老者。「給孩子報名嗎？」登記的小姐詢問他。

「不，給我自己報名。」老人回答說。小姐愕然的看著他。

老人解釋說：「我兒子在日本找了一個日本女孩做媳婦，他們每次回到家裡，都在我面前嘰哩咕嚕的講話。我一句也聽不懂。為了要跟他們交流，我希望能學日語。」

「你今年幾歲呢？」小姐問。

「68歲。」

「你想聽懂他們說的話，至少要學兩年啊。可是，兩年後你都已經70歲了耶。」

老人笑盈盈的反問道：「小姐，難道你以為我不學，兩年後會是66歲嗎？」

學習就是如此。我們往往以為自己開始得晚，而勸自己不要開始，不必嘗試。但是，其實不管我們是走著或是躺著，我們的年歲都會這樣年年增長的。只要開始，就永遠不會嫌晚。

　　老人學與不學之間的差別是：兩年之後，老人都一定會變成70歲，只不過，學了日語的老人能和兒媳們輕鬆對談，而沒有學日語的老人，卻只能呆站在一旁，有如木偶。

**相關諺語**

- It is never too old to learn.
  （學習永遠不嫌老。）

- You're never too old to learn.
  （學習永遠不嫌老。）

- It is never too late to learn.
  （學習永遠不嫌晚。）

- Learn young, learn fair; learn old, learn more.
  （少時學，學得好；老時學，學得多。）

### ※ 諺語單字補給站

| |
|---|
| **live** [lɪv] 活著 |
| **learn** [lɝn] 學會 |

**2**

# Knowledge is power.
**知識就是力量。**

---

**故事分享**

「Knowledge is power.」，知識對個人、對公司，都是相當重要的。

奇異公司旗下的美國設備融資公司總裁麥可‧派羅，曾經回憶起2004年之前，奇異公司蒐集潛在客戶的方法：

「我們靠蒐集電話簿、報紙、路上卡車車身上的公司標籤，或者建築物上的公司名稱，來建立公司的潛在客戶名單。」但是，從2004年開始，派羅認為奇異公司金融服務事業部應該改採科學的方法來做事。

科學的方法，就能為公司蒐集到更多的資訊，資訊蒐集的完整，就形成了一種專業的「知識」。

派羅要求業務經理列出潛在客戶的特性，他們利

用這些特性來分析哪些潛在客戶最有可能和他們做生意。

分析結果發現，其中六項特性和交易成功的關聯性最高。他們再進一步利用這六項指標，為所有潛在客戶進行評分，發現相當有利於銷售的評分結果：「排名前30％的潛在客戶跟我們交易的機率，比排在後面70％高三倍。」

從分析結果看來，科學的分析方法比傳統的舊式分類法，多篩選出了一萬名以上的優先客戶。可見，長久以來這一萬多名的優先客戶，都是公司行銷計畫的「遺珠」。

「知識就是力量」，因為奇異公司掌握的對客戶的正確知識，他們行銷的效率大大提升，也從此為公司賺得了更多的利潤。

 相關諺語

• A good book is a light to the soul.
（一本好書是靈魂之光。）

- Knowledge is a treasure but practice is the key to it.

  （知識是寶庫，而實踐是鑰匙。）

- Observation is the best teacher.

  （觀察是最佳良師。）

- Reading enriches the mind.

  （閱讀豐富了心靈。）

- Zeal without knowledge is fire without light.

  （熱心而無知，猶如無光之火。）

※ 諺語單字補給站

| |
| --- |
| **knowledge** [ˈnɑlɪdʒ] 知識 |
| **power** [ˈpauɚ] 力量 |
| **soul** [sol] 靈魂 |
| **treasure** [ˈtrɛʒɚ] 寶藏 |
| **observation** [ˌɑbzɚˈveʃən] 觀察 |
| **enrich** [ɪnˈrɪtʃ] 豐富了 |
| **zeal** [zil] 熱心 |

Part **4**

Appendix 附錄

## 3

# Art is long, life is short.
## 人生苦短，而學術無涯。

### 故事分享

統一集團高清愿董事長曾經說過，他終身的遺憾就是書唸的太少。高董事長因為家境的關係，所以，只讀到小學就沒有繼續求學了。

但是，任何一個想在人生有所成就的人，即使學歷不高，都仍然會藉著不斷學習，不斷充電，使人生散發光彩。

以世界500大企業的領頭羊之一波音公司為例，它極為注重員工的學習能力。

波音認為，如果你不具備學習能力，即使今天你再優秀，明天也可能會被淘汰。唯有靠「日日學習，日日進步」，一個人才能邁向成功。

半導體之父張忠謀也曾經說：「只有在你工作的前五年，你才用得到大學與研究所時代學到的20%到30%，之後的工作生涯中，用到你已經學會的東西的機會則等於零。因此，無論你是哪個行業的人，都要跟上潮流。」

因此，張忠謀先生利用吃早餐的時間看報紙，利用吃中餐的時間看枯燥的東西，諸如美國的思科、微軟的年報和資產負債表等等。

諾貝爾物理學獎得主楊振寧也是一個熱愛求知的人。他曾經發生過一次這樣的趣事：有一天，他到了圖書館看書，很快的他就完全進入了研究狀態，他完全忘記身邊的一切人、事、物，包括時間。

不知道經過了多久，圖書館的鈴聲響了好幾遍，管理員催促大家快點離開。但是，楊振寧因為太過於專心了，完全沒有意識到時間的流逝。就這樣，楊振寧在圖書館度過了一夜。相當珍惜時間的楊振寧，他的時間表當中沒有所謂的「節日、假日」，他長期的利用分分秒秒來做實驗，進行思考與演算，養成了一種充分利用時間來學習的習慣。

「Art is long, life is short.」這句話就是在提醒我們：只有不間斷的學習，才能和契機賽跑。只有不斷學習，才有機會「管理未來」。

### 相關諺語

- Future gains are uncertain.
  （活在當下。／別指望尚未實現的收益。）

- Read much, but not too many books.
  （多讀書，但不要讀很多書。）

- Books and friends should be few but good.
  （朋友與書，貴精不在多。）

- There is no royal road to learning.
  （學問無捷徑。）

※ 諺語單字補給站

| |
|---|
| **art** [ɑrt] 藝術、美術 |
| **long** [lɔŋ] 長久的 |
| **life** [laɪf] 生存、生命 |
| **short** [ʃɔrt] 短的 |

Part **4**

Appendix 附錄

**4**

# It is easy to be wise after the event.

經一事長一智。

## 故事分享

問題越大，機會往往越大。

第一個聞名全球的台灣話是什麼呢？是台語「免削（Bensia）」。這一切，就開始於一個疼女兒的爸爸所遭遇的小難題。

洪勉之是一個疼愛女兒的父親。他的女兒跟他說：「爸！幫我多削幾隻鉛筆啦。同學阿明、阿華的鉛筆盒都是滿滿的一堆削得尖尖的鉛筆，尖的鉛筆寫字比較漂亮，你才削幾隻，很快就都鈍了啦。」

當天晚上，洪勉之為了心愛的女兒獨自一個人在削鉛筆，他突然靈光一閃：「如果能夠把削好的鉛筆芯放在一個空管子裡面，寫鈍一支就抽一支出來，是不是就很方便呢？」就這樣，他想出了「免削鉛筆」的

創意。

一九六〇年，洪勉之把這個創意以八百萬的天價賣給了紡織大亨莊金池先生，五年之後，行銷全世界的免削鉛筆誕生了。因為這個創意價值驚人，大英百科全書還因此收錄了「Bensia」這句台灣話。

問題大，機會就大。如果沒有經一事，你如何能夠「長一智」？

好點子，通常就是來自於對現狀的不滿。瑪莎史都華，美國知名雜誌創辦人，她的油漆產品就是這樣誕生出來的。

瑪莎平常就時常觀察生活中許多大自然顏色，在她想要裝潢自己家裡的幾個房間時，她就發現自己到處也找不到那些可以與天然色澤比擬的油漆色澤。

為了解決這個問題，瑪莎必須與她的創業夥伴們合作，取材於大自然，調製出與大自然相仿的獨特色澤。

於是，瑪莎從一群稀有的雞所生的蛋開始取材，這些蛋有些是精緻的蛋白色，有些有濃鬱的奶油色，另外也能產生出特殊的米黃色。

　　甚至，有一種叫做阿勞卡那（Araucana）的母雞，可以產出淺藍綠色的蛋，顏色美麗極了。

　　這些顏色在一般油漆店中根本就找不到。瑪莎和她的團隊因為遭遇這樣的問題，因此設計出獨特、漂亮的，超過400種的新顏色。這些顏色與瑪莎史都華的家飾、傢俱搭配起來，更顯得美麗。

　　因此，當你遭遇問題的時候，請勿慌張，這也是你發現另一條出路的捷徑。

　　「It is easy to be wise after the event.」問題發生之前，你很難聰明的意識到這個問題。一旦問題出現過了，再次遇到時，你就能坦然以對。

### 相關諺語

- Necessity is the mother of invention.
  （需要為發明之母。）

- Take away the cause, and the effect must cease.
  （沒有因，哪有果。）

- Thought is the seed of action.
  （思想為行動之種子。）

- Experience keeps a dear school.
  （經驗是最佳教育。）

- Experience must be bought.
  （必須付出代價學到經驗。）

※ 諺語單字補給站

| |
|---|
| **easy** [ˈizɪ] 容易的，不費力的 |
| **wise** [waɪz] 有智慧的，聰明的 |
| **after** [ˈæftɚ] 在……之後 |
| **event** [ɪˈvɛnt] 事件、大事 |

## 5

# It is never too late to mend.

**亡羊補牢猶未晚也。**

### 故事分享

　　人非聖賢，孰能無過？TVBS這家新聞媒體，就曾經犯下多種錯誤，播出諸多的烏龍報導。TVBS曾經報導：台灣的許多食用鴨隻的除毛過程，有可能是用瀝青除毛的。一夕之間，全國消費者都聞鴨色變，薑母鴨的生意掉了一半以上。

　　薑母鴨的業者反映說：「以前冬天銷售量好像冬天進補，生意很好耶！現在生意少了一半以上！」

　　為了彌補這樣的傷害，TVBS特地在台中舉辦免費品嘗薑母鴨的活動。活動當時，許多來吃免費薑母鴨的民眾都說，當時看到TVBS的報導，確實讓他們不敢吃鴨，店家的生意因此大受影響。為了彌補當初的過錯，TVBS特地請來衛生局長掛保證，證實所有鴨

隻都是經過檢驗，完全沒有瀝青鴨。民眾在這樣的活動當中，大口大口的吃鴨，20隻番鴨煮成的薑母鴨瞬間就被吃光了。

台灣媒體報錯新聞的何其多，但是能夠如此負責任的做一些彌補行動的，卻是少數。就算是微不足道的彌補，一點點付出，也不能被磨滅。

「It is never too late to mend.」，任何企業或個人，都不該在犯下錯誤之後，不負責的逃避責任。他們應該努力的朝向彌補過錯的方向去做。即使短時間看來，你並沒有成功，你並未為公司賺得財富，但是只要開始努力，何時都不嫌晚。

有一個年輕人，好不容易獲得了一份銷售員的工作。但是，他勤懇的做了大半年的努力，卻還是在幾個重大案子中頻頻失誤，他的同事個個都做得很出色，他心中忍不住感到很慚愧。

於是，年輕人走入總經理的辦公室，他慚愧的說：我可能不適合這個工作。

「安心的做吧！我會給你足夠的時間，直到你成功為止。到了那時候，你再想走，我也不會留你的。」

老總的寬容，讓年輕人相當感動。他決定再努力一陣子，做出成績再走。

於是，年輕人多了一些冷靜、思考的態度，兢兢業業的繼續在工作上努力。

過了一年之後，年輕人再次進入總經理的辦公室。和上次不同的是，他已經連續七個月在銷售業績排行榜上面高居榜首，成了當之無愧的業務高手。原來，這份工作如此適合自己！但是，他想親口問問老總，為何當初老總會願意繼續留用自己呢？

「因為，我比你更不甘心。」老總解釋說：「徵人時，公司收到一百多份應徵資料，我從中挑選了二十多人面試，最後，我甚至只錄取了你一個人。如果接受你的辭職，我就是失敗了。我深信，既然面試時你可以打敗對手，得到我的認可，那麼我相信你一定也能在工作中得到客戶的認同的。你缺少的，只是機會與時間。與其說我對你有信心，不如說我對自己仍有信心，我相信自己不會看錯人。」

「It is never too late to mend.」，只要能夠彌補自己的過錯，都不該嫌晚！如果你今天暫時沒有獲得成

功，現在就開始彌補，仍然可以像故事裡的業務員那樣讓人刮目相看的。

相關諺語

- It is never too late to apologize.
  （道歉不嫌晚。）

- Let bygones be bygones.
  （既往不咎。）

- Kind words soften anger.
  （好聽的話使怒氣緩和。）

※ 諺語單字補給站

| | |
|---|---|
| **late** [let] 遲的，晚的 | |
| **mend** [mɛnd] 修補 | |

## 6

# No pains, no gains.
**不勞則無獲。**

---

**故事分享**

流著汗水歡欣灑種，就能夠歡笑收割。只要能夠學習忍受痛苦，品嘗成功果實的機會就不遠了。

羅曼・羅蘭曾說：「人生，原本就是痛苦的。不要詛咒人生的痛苦，應該在苦痛中學習、修養、覺悟，在苦痛中發現我們內蘊的寶藏。」

在每個家庭的廚房當中，難免都會有許多的油污。我的家庭也不例外，家裡廚房中這些各式各樣的油污，用普通的清潔劑也不容易清除。

有一天，在電視上突然看到了清理油污的小妙招。先用清潔劑噴在油污上方之後，覆蓋上保鮮膜，確保清潔劑完全附著在油污上，然後再用吹風機的熱氣吹著髒污的局部。

　　吹了熱氣的油污，輕輕用抹布一擦，往往就變得很乾淨。

　　後來，我還把這個原理應用在清洗平底鍋。平底鍋洗過之後，裝上一些自來水，煮滾之後熄火，側面一看，就會看到一層薄薄的油污漂浮在這些滾水的水面。這樣一來，平底鍋就會徹底的乾淨了。

　　油污，就像是每個人的殘缺性格，熱氣、熱水，就像是人生的考驗與困境。只有夠熱的熱氣，才能清除掉這些油污；只有夠痛苦的考驗，才能幫助我們粹煉出更好的人格；只有品嘗過苦果，才懂得享受成功的甜味。

　　沒有痛苦，就沒有收穫！沒有考驗，就沒有芬芳。王海波就曾經說過：「來得太容易的東西，絕對不會是好的。」當挫折成為過去，會變成是美好的成長經驗。人生裡，有太多曾經讓我們痛不欲生的失敗經驗：考試沒有錄取、被老闆炒魷魚、投資慘敗、戀人要求分手、甚至親人驟然離世……。事過境遷以後，傷口結痂了，我們都將因痛苦而重生。

　　挫折只是一時，成長卻是永遠。「No pains, no gains.（不勞則無獲。）」，與其忘記挫折，不如堅定自己努力的方向，舉起我們下沉的疲軟的手臂，朝目標繼續奮鬥。不要白白受挫折，而是積極把挫折轉化為成功的動力，將挫折化做成長的養分，現在就開始茁壯吧。

**相關諺語**

- He that can't endure the bad will not live to see the good.
  （無法撐過苦境，無法看到美地。）

- He who risks nothing gains nothing.
  （不入虎穴，焉得虎子。）

- No cross, no crown.
  （沒有痛苦十字架，哪來榮耀冠冕。）

- Nothing ventured nothing gained.
  （無冒險無所獲。／不入虎穴，焉得虎子。）

- Pleasure comes through toil.
  （苦盡甘來。）

※ 諺語單字補給站

**pain** [pen] 痛苦

**gain** [gen] 收穫

## 7

# Nothing ventured, nothing gained.

**不入虎穴，焉得虎子。**

---

**故事分享**

　　電影《氣象人》當中，尼可拉斯·凱吉飾演的角色曾經說過一句話：「你知道嗎？難做的事和應該做的事，往往是同一件事？凡是有意義的事情都不容易。在成年人的生活裡，沒有『容易』兩個字。」

　　在這部電影中，尼卡拉斯·凱吉飾演的主角大衛，是一個典型的中年男人。他不滿意他自己的事業、擁有糟糕的婚姻，兩個看似聽話卻問題不斷的青少年孩子，以及頗有聲望且不斷對自己造成壓力的患病父親。這一切問題糾纏混雜在一起，問題都看似不大，卻百般糾纏著主角大衛。

　　天氣預報員的生活就像這句台詞一樣，看不到「容易」兩個字。我們和他也相距不遠，我們也許也一

樣，面對挑戰，有點勇敢自負，卻又有點退縮；容易幻想，不善表達，時常把事情搞砸。

另一部電影《刺激一九九五》，卻有著令人震撼的一句警語：「一開始你排斥它，後來你習慣它，只要時間夠久，你最後會變得離不開它。這就是體制化。」

人是有惰性的動物，一旦適應了一種體制，離開了就會很不適應。在《刺激一九九五》這部電影中，服刑五十年的布魯克斯竟然開始習慣監獄，甚至想以傷害同伴的做法留在監獄當中。生活中，往往我們也不斷再重複著這種模式：鋒芒畢露，然後墨守成規，從抵制、不滿，逐漸變成委曲求全。

日復一日被同化的我們，就算有短瞬間的靈光一閃，意識到什麼常規之外的路徑，我們卻已經無法再做任何改變了。

但人生是需要冒險的。「Nothing ventured, nothing gained.」，沒有冒險，怎麼能挑戰自我，好收穫甜美的果實？不入虎穴，焉得虎子。機會來臨的時候，我們缺乏的不是能力，而是跳出框架的勇氣。

Part **4**

Appendix 附錄

**相關諺語**

- Adversity leads to prosperity.
  （逆境導致成功。）

- No pleasure without pain.
  （沒有苦，就沒有樂。）

- No gain without pain.
  （不勞無獲。）

- Distress offers opportunities for the obtaining of success.
  （生於憂患，死於安樂。）

## ※ 諺語單字補給站

| |
|---|
| **nothing** [ˈnʌθɪŋ] 沒什麼事 |
| **venture** [ˈvɛntʃɚ] 冒險 |
| **have** [hæv] 擁有 |
| **adversity** [ədˈvɝsətɪ] 逆境、厄運 |
| **prosperity** [prɑsˈpɛrətɪ] 繁榮、繁華 |
| **distress** [dɪˈstrɛs] 悲痛、苦惱 |
| **offer** [ˈɔfɚ] 提供 |

**8**

# Actions speak louderthan words.

坐而言，不如起而行。

---

### 故事分享

　　想要鼓勵別人「積極採取行動」嗎？這句英語諺語可以鼓勵身邊的人，不只是有想法，還能立刻採取行動。

　　雷根曾是一名演員，可是他卻非常想當總統。從22歲到54歲，雷根從電臺體育播音員，到好萊塢電影明星，將自己整個青年到中年的歲月，都投入演藝圈了，政治對他來說完全是陌生的，更別說會有任何經驗了。

　　雖然雷根從政的阻礙很多。然而，當機會來臨，雷根因為擔任通用電氣公司的電視節目主持人，開始深入瞭解社會各層面以及社會大眾的心聲。當共和黨內和保守派和一些富豪們竭力慫恿他競選加州州長時，雷根毅然放棄大半輩子賴以為生的演藝事業，下定決

心打算開闢人生的新領域。最後，他甚至達到「美國總統」這個政治的最高峰。

假如雷根只是擁有一個美好的夢想，但是從來沒有去完成過，那麼他的夢想永遠只能是一個夢想。而當一個人實際的採取行動時，就可以讓夢想成真，品嘗甜美的果實。希望這個句子能讓你重拾你的夢想，開始採取行動。

在英文當中，「採取行動」叫做take actions。所以，如果你從來不曾take actions，你的構思就永遠只是一個無形的構思。當你終於開始採取行動之後，你就距離夢想越來越近了。

在「Actions speak louder than words.」這句話中，「行動」是擬人化的，其實，現實生活中也是如此。知道嗎？你的行動會說話。如果你口口聲聲都是「愛與付出」，面對受傷的人，你卻從未扶他們一把，那你的言語也只不過是造假而已。

相反的，如果你不太會說話，但當你身邊的人有需要時，你總是默默的伸出手來幫助他們，你的愛與真誠，總有一天會被人理解的。行動所能表達的也絕對比言語所能表達的還多。

**相關諺語**

- No sooner said than done.
  （劍及履及。／說了要馬上做。）

- A little help is worth a (great) deal of pity.
  （口惠不如實惠。）

- A man apt to promise is apt to forget.
  （小人好允諾。）

※ 諺語單字補給站

| |
|---|
| **actions** ['ækʃəns] 行動 |
| **speak** [spik] 說 |
| **louder** ['laʊdə] 更大聲 |
| **than** [ðæn] 比較 |
| **words** ['wɝdz] 話語 |
| **take** [tek] 採取 |

Part **4**

Appendix

附錄

**9**

# First come first served.
捷足先登。

---
### 故事分享

　　人生就好比一場賽跑，你越快開始朝目標前進，你就有更大的獲勝機會。

　　如果永遠都只會「跟風」，你的機會很可能就已經消失了。試想一下：石頭怎樣才能在水上漂起來呢？把石頭掏空嗎？成本太大！把石頭放在木板上嗎？未必有木板！只有靠一種力量：速度。速度夠快的石頭，才能在水面上飛起來。

　　《孫子兵法》有一句話說：「激水之疾，至於漂石者，勢也。」速度決定了石頭能否漂起來。人生也是如此，沒有人為你等待，也沒有機會為你停留，你只有與時間賽跑，才有可能會贏。如果說，成功也有捷徑的話，那就是飛，而尚未起飛之前，要時刻準備

飛。

「First come first served.」這句話，應用在商場上更是如此。面對中國大陸這個龐大的新興市場，來自美國的知名的全美傢俱企業Home Depot雖然也想有所斬獲，但是比起來自英國的Kingfisher，卻已經遲到很久了。遲到的門票是昂貴的，Home Depot因此在2006年以1億美元的代價，收購位於天津的「家世界」(Home Way)傢俱超市，試著挽救4 %市佔率的頹勢，想辦法追上英國Kingfisher 20%的市佔率。

成功的人，都是最快掌握時勢和資訊的人。只有加快自己吸收、學習的速度，你才能在知識經濟的時代中站穩一席之地。

我們再來看「First come first served.」這句知名的諺語，這整個句子其實省略了當主詞的關係代名詞、先行詞和動詞，然後整個句子變成倒裝句。

**The one who come first will be served first.**

請看上面的句子，這樣才算是個完整的英文句子，主詞、動詞都不缺。但是實際上，講英文卻不需要這樣，只要能夠彼此瞭解意思，不至於誤會，就算是成

功的表達了。在學習英文的路上，當然也是越早開始越好。開始開口說你的第一句英文，就已經朝「和老外輕鬆對話」又近了一步了。

**相關諺語**

- Early sow, early mow.
  （早播種，早收成。）

- An hour in the morning is worth two in the evening.
  （一日之計在於晨。）

- Every minute counts.
  （分秒必爭。）

- He that will thrive must rise at five.
  （想成功的人必須早起。）

- He that rises late must trot all day.
  （晚起床的人，整日匆忙。）

- No morning sun lasts a whole day.
  （晨光不久留，好花不常開。）

- The early bird catches the worm.
  （早起的鳥兒有蟲吃。）

※ 諺語單字補給站

| |
| --- |
| **first** [fɜst] 第一的 |
| **come** [kʌm] 來 |
| **served** [sɜv] 被服事的 |
| **depot** [dɪpo] 倉庫 |
| **kingfisher** [ˈkɪŋˌfɪʃɚ] 翠鳥 |
| **way** [we] 風俗、習慣、作風 |

Part 4

Appendix 附錄

英語系列：28

# 英語寫作滿分特訓

主編／施銘瑋
作者／Craig Sorenson
譯者／張中倩
出版者／哈福企業有限公司
地址／新北市中和區景新街 347 號 11 樓之 6
電話／(02) 2945-6285　傳真／(02) 2945-6986
郵政劃撥／31598840　戶名／哈福企業有限公司
出版日期／2016 年 4 月
定價／NT$ 249 元（附 MP3）

全球華文國際市場總代理／采舍國際有限公司
地址／新北市中和區中山路 2 段 366 巷 10 號 3 樓
電話／(02) 8245-8786　傳真／(02) 8245-8718
網址／www.silkbook.com　新絲路華文網

香港澳門總經銷／和平圖書有限公司
地址／香港柴灣嘉業街 12 號百樂門大廈 17 樓
電話／(852) 2804-6687　傳真／(852) 2804-6409
定價／港幣 83 元（附 MP3）

視覺設計／Wan Wan
內文排版／Jo Jo
email／haanet68@Gmail.com

郵撥打九折，郵撥未滿 500 元，酌收 1 成運費，
滿 500 元以上者免運費

國家圖書館出版品預行編目資料

英語寫作滿分特訓 / 施銘瑋◎主編 Craig Sorenson◎ 著
.張中倩◎譯 -- 新北市：哈福企業, 2016.04
　　面；　公分. --（英語系列；28）
　ISBN 978-986-5616-53-3(平裝附光碟片)

1.英語 2.讀本

805.1892　　　　　　　　　　　　　105003908

哈福

哈福